AND OTHER FAIRY TALES

JEANNA MASON STAY

Copyright © 2026 by Jeanna Mason Stay

All rights reserved.

No portion of this book may be reproduced in any form without written permission from the publisher or author, except as permitted by U.S. copyright law.

Cover design by Ana Cruz
anacruzarts.com

Tosscobble Publishing logo, interior art, and edge design by Addra Stay
Edge printing by Ashley Bustamante

Unknown

I AM NOT EXPECTING it when I round the outcropping of stone on this windswept beach, but there it is, sharp and sudden and stark. It gapes before me, this sudden grotto, and beckons me enter.

Is it filled with treasure—rubies and sapphires rising in mounds to the ceiling, wealth beyond imagination? Or does a dragon dwell within, slumbering, waiting to destroy the one who dares disturb it?

It might hold both.

I stand at the entrance, squinting, hoping for a glimpse of my unknown future.

And I think I won't go in just yet.

Table of Contents

1. Unknown — 1
2. Unspeakable Sweaters — 3
3. The Elf and the Fisherman — 35
4. Diamonds and Pearls — 39
5. Forged in Iron and Blood — 43
6. The Nanny Job — 65
7. Daughters of Sea — 73
8. Some Restrictions Apply — 75
9. Song and Storm — 79
10. The Promise of Snow — 103
11. The Candlemaker — 121
12. Breadcrumbs — 133
13. The Cinderella Plan — 147
14. A Selection of Documents — 151
15. Wolfskin — 171
16. Siren's Younger Sister — 175
17. Spun from Linen and Lies — 181
18. Sharp and Pointy Teeth — 231

19. To Dance with the Fae	235
Story Notes	238
Acknowledgments and Kickstarter Thank Yous	243
About the Author	246

Unspeakable Sweaters

NOVEMBER. Thanksgiving, to be exact.
Fact: Every curse requires a loophole. Bad for contract lawyers, good for magical victims.

It all started with my stepmother. I should have known she would be a problem. If fairy tales had taught me nothing else, they at least proved that men had terrible taste in second wives.

But my six younger brothers and I had all flown the coop by the time Dad remarried, so it never occurred to me to worry that maybe she wasn't just a stepmother, but an Evil Stepmother (an ES, for short). Besides, I didn't believe in witches.

Clearly I should have.

It had already been an awful Thanksgiving. Dad had died the previous year. Mysteriously? I didn't think so at the time. He was really big on holidays though; he'd made us all come back and visit every year. Now he was gone, but it felt wrong not to get together for Thanksgiving. The twins were finishing their senior year at UMBC, and the rest of us still lived in the area. So it would be our last holiday all together in the Baltimore condo complex where we'd grown up, before the ES sold it off and moved to Florida. It was a turning point, the end of an era. We had to honor Dad one final time.

None of us expected anything worse than overcooked turkey, dry stuffing, and a hefty dose of awkwardness. All standard Thanksgiving fare.

In retrospect, maybe I shouldn't blame everything on the ES. It was Joseph, after all, who had the brilliant idea to hold a burping contest. I love my brothers, but honestly? They'd all hit their mid-twenties and still acted like teenagers. I rolled my eyes and sighed. No wonder none of them were married yet.

As we sat around the ES's antique mahogany table and the burping began, she gritted her teeth and started clearing the dishes. Her fuse was probably already short after Jake (or maybe James? It was sometimes hard to keep any of them straight, but the twins especially) had spilled a pre-dinner drink on her chaise longue.

I elbowed Jared in the ribs (my parents really loved their J names) and looked pointedly at the china left on the table. This was my first tactical error.

He took the hint and stood up. "Hey, ES, let me help you." I inwardly groaned. Yes, we jokingly called her the ES amongst ourselves, but right to her face? I wanted to smack him.

She glared at him like she knew he was being insulting but didn't know exactly how.

"Oh," I rushed to say, "that's our nickname for you. It stands for…" I looked around the table, hoping one of the others would rescue me.

When Jack opened his mouth, I realized I shouldn't have looked to them for rescue. They'd probably be happy to tell her what the name meant.

So I cut in faster. "It stands for Emilia Sweetie." I grinned widely. "Because, you know, you're so sweet, and we love you so much."

"Uh, yeah, what Kelly said," Jared agreed halfheartedly.

She looked at me in silence, her fist clenched around a washrag. The moment stretched, but a loud honk from the traffic outside snapped the tension, and she turned back to the sink.

In the meantime, James (or Jake?) had decided that now was the time to join the fray. He picked up an unused saucer and tossed it from hand to hand. Seriously, my brothers were such little boys.

"Yo, over here," Jared called.

As James lobbed the fine china saucer across the table, the world seemed to slip into slow motion. The saucer flew in a perfect arc toward Jared.

And straight through Jared's fumbling hands.

The china shattered on the hardwood floor. Then I made my second tactical error of the evening. I jumped up and rushed to the ES. I put a conciliatory hand on her shoulder, trying to shield my stupid brothers from her wrath. "Oh, Emilia, I'm so sorry. I'm sure they are too."

I glared at them both until they muttered their apologies, and turned back to her. "Now why don't you go sit down and rest while I clean up and—"

"No," the ES shouted, hands on her hips. "No more." She pointed an accusatory finger at each of them. "I'm tired of all of you! This is the last straw."

I gaped. Of everything they'd ever done to her, *this* was when she'd finally had enough? "They're really sorry," I said. "They're just a little birdbrained—"

She turned on me. "And you—always protecting them. Well, let's see how well you protect them now."

This was where things got weird.

Her skin began to glow—not the makeup counter sort of glow, more of the transforming-into-a-Disney-villain glow. Her voice took on an echoing quality, and she started spouting poetry.

At first all I noticed was the terrible rhyming and meter. Somewhere Dr. Seuss was rolling in his grave. But then the meaning of her words penetrated the fog of iambic-ish tetrameter.

The ES apparently agreed with the whole birdbrained bit, except she carried it one step further: birdbodied. Pigeons, to be exact. Sure, swans were more traditional for this sort of thing, but who ever heard of urban swans?

Wind swept around my brothers. They sprouted feathers. They squawked. They shrank. They pecked crumbs off the floor.

I gaped in horror, my brain stuttering, refusing to wrap itself around what I saw. This had to be some crazy bad-turkey-induced nightmare.

The ES smiled in satisfaction and turned toward me.

With the way my heart pounded, I felt *very* awake.

I backed away and opened my mouth to protest before she could do anything to me, but the ES interrupted. "I wouldn't, if I were you."

The bad poetry continued.

I could hardly process anything at the time, but something about listening to a life-altering curse kind of brands the words in your memory, so I had plenty of time to think about it all later.

If lousy rhymes like "break the spell" and "they'll get tall" were to be believed, I was in some sort of fairy tale curse loophole. My brothers were doomed to never-ending birdhood... unless I saved them, of course. And how could I save them? So glad you asked.

I had a year (seven years was more traditional, but rising magical costs, curse hyperinflation, blah blah blah). And in that year I had to go mute. No talking. No communication of any kind about the curse. I also had to knit six stinging nettle shirts, all by hand, completely from scratch, using only locally sourced, ethically grown materials.

The really fun part was that there were no take-backsies. Make a mistake and yell in traffic? Bam, birds forever. Don't finish the shirts in time? I'd be looking at a good decade or two of pigeon ownership and a crushing guilt complex.

Things like this didn't happen in real life, did they? I was pretty sure I hadn't read any headlines lately about bird curses or freaky glowing stepmothers.

But the evidence was before me, and with dread I realized I couldn't deny what had just happened and what would happen next.

I would have to learn to knit.

NOVEMBER (still). Thanksgiving/Black Friday.
Fact: In magical curses, as in bureaucracy, even loopholes have loopholes.

I had nothing left to say after that. Literally.

So with a supremely unsatisfactory glare in the ES's direction, I shooed my brothers out the door. Luring them into the back of my rusty little Honda Civic turned out to be a bit trickier (and I got a lot of weird stares from pedestrians), but I finally managed it once I found a half-empty bag of stale potato chips on the floor in the backseat. With my squawking passengers safely pecking away behind me, I drove home, mulling over the words of the ES's spell and looking for further loopholes.

I wasn't sure what talking had to do with knitting or breaking curses, but clearly I didn't make the rules. So talking was out. And anything about the curse was out. But the ES conveniently hadn't said anything about emails or texts on other topics. With the internet, who needed speech anyway? I would be fine, at least when it came to *that* part of the curse.

I pulled into the dim parking lot behind my brownstone and checked out the chaos in the backseat. How was I going to get them inside? And where was I going to put them when I did? Ten minutes, several pillowcases, and a lot more potato chips later, and I had them all safely ensconced in my postage-stamp-sized bathroom. That was going to be a problem when I needed to shower, but right then all I cared about was keeping them off the carpet.

I grabbed my laptop to do some research. First order of business: cages, birdseed, whatever other pet-owning supplies I now had to acquire. Probably a permit of some sort. I was pretty sure pigeons were legal in the city. At least I hoped so. The nettles and knitting would have to wait.

I woke up the next morning with my forehead pressed onto my laptop keyboard, the screen black since I'd forgotten to plug it in. I scrubbed my face with my hands, trying to make my brain remember why I'd fallen asleep like that. Suddenly I sat up with a pop, all the memories from the night before flooding back in. Oh. The curse.

Double oh. My brothers.

I ran to the bathroom and opened the door. The place was like a horror show of shredded toilet paper and bird poop. I opened my mouth to yell at them, then clapped my hands over my lips. Less than twenty-four hours and I'd already almost blown it.

I slammed the door shut, scrounged up some stale bread and leftover salad, and shoved that through the bathroom door. Hopefully pet supply shops had Black Friday sales.

NOVEMBER (yes, still).
Fact: YouTube. It's not quite magic, but it's close.

I sat swaddled in a fluffy comforter, fuzzy socks on my feet, staring at my computer screen. Again. It turned out that pet stores did indeed have Black Friday sales and I was now the proud owner of pigeon paraphernalia aplenty. One of my brothers (Joseph, probably, though they all *still* looked alike to me) squawked at the top of his lungs from inside his brand-new cage out on my enclosed back porch. It was late at night, so he was probably breaking some sort of noise ordinance.

Joseph squawked again, and one of the neighbors yelled a few choice words out the window.

I couldn't even yell back, "Sorry."

After nearly yelling at my brothers no fewer than twelve times over the last few hours, I'd decided I needed a little help until I got better at remembering the whole "no talking" thing. I couldn't fail my curse-breaking gig in the first week. I stretched several strips of tape over my mouth, then cringed when it tugged at my skin. Maybe I should let my brothers fly free. The idea was tempting. They would go away and I could speak again and my neighbors would go back to cheerfully ignoring me.

I sighed. No, I couldn't do that. They were crazy making, but they were mine.

I stared at my computer screen again. Now that I had the pigeon living situation reasonably settled, it was time to dive into the curse.

I typed "how to make nettle yarn" into Google and watched the results scroll. Brilliant!

The ES's spell had given me a year, but surely that was an overestimate. After all, if so many people before me had posted all about the process, how hard could it possibly be?

Collect a little nettle. Sort of... twist it up somehow into yarn. A little knitting (after the minor detail of learning to knit in the first place). And voila. My brothers would be human again by New Year's. Valentine's at the latest. No problem.

Of course, they'd still be annoying and loud and now jobless and homeless and probably living with me forever because no sane person would ever marry them and I was free rent.

But at least they'd be human, and I'd be free to return to my life as an underappreciated thirty-something data entry clerk paying too much for a tiny, subpar brownstone in an unsavory end of Baltimore. A regular happily ever after. Ish.

I created a spreadsheet and typed away, figuring supplies and costs, laying out a timeline, and calculating the hours it would take. I clicked on one of the many nettle-related videos on the internet, this one of an enthusiastic woman with a messy bun walking through a sunlit field. I typed notes as she explained how to collect stinging nettles without, you know, being stung (that was a relief; even *thinking* about poison ivy gave me hives). She brought them home and quickly took us through the process of retting, drying, breaking, pulling the fibers, and spinning.

The longer the video went on, the longer my notes got, and the less enthusiastic I felt. *Her* enthusiasm never waned, though. She was perky to the last cut. "And that's how I got from this"—a still photo of a monstrous pile of nettle plants—"to this." She held three small lumpy balls of yarn.

I swallowed.

Maybe I needed to aim for Mother's Day instead.

DECEMBER/JANUARY/FEBRUARY/INTERMINABLY SLUDGY BALTIMORE WINTER WITH BAD HOUSEHOLD VENTILATION.

Fact: It is not romantic to live with woodland creatures. They smell. They eat. A lot. They never clean up after themselves.

Mother's Day wasn't possible either. I'd be lucky—insanely lucky—if I managed to break the spell at all, with even minutes to spare.

Stupid stinging nettles. Large quantities weren't even harvestable until August and September. A little in July, if the weather was right. I'd have only a few months to do all the collecting and spinning and knitting.

I looked wearily at the spreadsheet I'd created on my computer, with columns for time spent in all the stages that would lead me to a final product. Suddenly the whole madness of this business felt overwhelming. How was I going to manage this?

I took a deep breath. One tiny step at a time.

I couldn't collect the nettles themselves until August, but I had plenty of stuff to learn before then. I was training for a marathon, that's how I saw it. I wouldn't be running the real race until later, but for now, I would prepare. There were skills to be acquired! Supplies to be purchased! Finger calluses to form!

I got up and stretched. Enough agonizing over the spreadsheet for now. I might as well agonize over something else instead. I grabbed a quick bite of leftover Chinese food, went out and tossed some bird feed to my brothers, then sat on my couch to watch my millionth YouTube knitting video of the month.

With cheap acrylic yarn, I spent the next hour trying to force my hands, fingers, and knitting needles to do what looked so simple when someone else did it. Fretting about my inability to knit kept me from drowning in the despair of everything else I had to do. Rotational hopelessness was the way to go.

MARCH (AND KINDA, SORTA APRIL).
Fact: Even fairy tale heroines need a voice.

A sad truth of life is that if you stop talking and take a sudden obsessive interest in knitting, your friends are unlikely to understand. None of them believed me when I wrote that it was important but wouldn't explain why. When I kept silent week after week, most of my friends simply... moved on.

On the other hand, my coworkers didn't really care (we'd never been close in the first place) and my boss didn't even notice. Which was fortunate, because I really needed job security with all my weird new expenses. So I guess there were benefits to having a lousy job with minimal human interactions.

I wasn't in touch with the ES (obviously), and while my brothers lived on the back porch, they weren't great conversationalists. I still didn't know if they could understand anything I gestured at them. Gnawing on stale pizza crusts and scratching awkwardly were pretty much the only responses I got from them when they were human too, so I wasn't sure how much had changed.

It only took me a few months of this curse-imposed silence to realize I was going to literally lose my mind if I didn't do something about it. I needed an outlet. Not speaking for a few days could be a fun experiment, but months on end was getting ugly.

The answer to my dilemma seemed obvious. Where do the voiceless go when they have something to say? The internet, of course.

So naturally I started a TikTok.

I set my phone on its cheap tripod, pressed record, and sat back on my tattered couch to show off my latest attempt at knitting. It looked more like a zombie snake than the lovely soft scarf from the pattern, but I was getting better. My first scarf looked like Cthulhu risen from the abyss.

Once I'd recorded everything, I spent a few minutes adding captions and went to my account, SartorialExperiment_4_6. The fine print of the curse suggested I couldn't explain *why* I was doing anything, but that didn't mean I couldn't "talk" about it at least a little. So I did.

I even made it educational when I could. It turned out stinging nettles weren't as bad as they sound. Nettle leaves were edible and nutritious. Yarn made from nettle fibers was quite soft (when spun by someone with actual skill, AKA not me). I was pretty sure the ES hadn't known that when she placed the curse, and I couldn't help gloating at the small ways in which her plotting had been foiled. Even the harvesting wasn't horrible, if you were careful.

My TikToks all looked like they belonged on Pinterest Fails, but oh well. It was, at least, an outlet.

After I uploaded my latest video, I spent a few minutes staring at my stats, which were distressingly low. I didn't care about the popularity of my account, except for one thing—I needed it for networking.

Networking had never been my thing, but I now found myself in critical need of friends. Friends with giant fields of nettles, the bigger the better. Friends who might share their fields of nettles. I was hoping that I could use my platform to find these friends, assuming there were such people.

MAY.

Fact: People will always find their community. Weird attachment to collectible spoons? There's a Reddit for that. Absolute fascination with creepy bathrooms? Join the Facebook group. There is a flock for everyone.

Before the curse, I hadn't even known festivals like this existed. Everything I knew about natural fibers I'd learned from the tags of my t-shirts. Clothing was not the sort of thing you made by hand. Or if you did, you at least bought the materials with Amazon Prime.

After the curse, when I'd started attending meetups of fiber enthusiasts, I discovered there were whole swaths of people who found camaraderie in discussing yarns and dyes and Ashford traddy versus Kromski spinning wheels. This notion was just as foreign to me as spells cast by evil stepmothers and brothers being turned into pigeons. Yet here I was, under the brilliant spring sky, attending the largest natural fibers festival in the Delmarva region.

An entire festival. Devoted to natural fibers.

The world was an amazing place.

I strolled to yet another display booth, my eyes wandering over the brightly colored yarns and threads (all hand-dyed, of course) arrayed before me. They were beautiful, but one glance at the price tags told me I'd be sticking to the cheap stuff.

I hoped I would find some more connections who had nettle fields here, but even more, I needed to get a handle on spinning. I'd watched a million YouTube videos and tried it myself at home, but nothing came out right. I cursed the existence of all things spindle-y. I clearly needed some hands-on help.

One booth down, a group of starry-eyed teens and older women giggled and crowded around something I couldn't see. Out of curiosity, I scooted closer until I caught a glimpse of the center of their attention. A man sat on a stool, dropping and spinning a little wooden spindle. The sun glinted off his short black curls, and when he smiled, the right corner of his mouth revealed a delicious dimple. Suddenly, I could see the appeal of spinning your own yarn. Someone in the group spoke, and the man nodded. I didn't hear his reply, but I was certain it was clever.

I drew closer. A drop spindle—exactly what I needed to learn about.

Which was the only reason I was drawn into this circle. Not at all because I, like the feminine hordes around me, suddenly felt a little starry eyed.

I was close enough now to hear the man's deep chuckle. I was definitely warming to the world of drop spindles.

I elbowed a pretty blonde twenty-something out of the way to get a better view. It was all in the spirit of education. Not because of the dimple or the smile or the biceps revealed through the man's close-fitting t-shirt.

"So when the fiber breaks like this"—he purposely let the spindle drop to the ground—"you just stretch out the fibers here." He demonstrated weaving the fibers back together. "Add in the new fibers and keep spinning. Just keep spinning, just keep spinning," he said in a sing-song voice.

The girls all tittered.

So did I. Silently, of course.

Wait, what? Thirty-ahem-year-olds do *not* titter.

The girls thanked him for the demonstration and moved on.

He looked up from his spindle straight at me and smiled.

My heart most emphatically did *not* skip a beat.

"Hi there," he said, reaching down to grab another tuft of wool. "Anything I can do for you? Need a drop spindle demo?"

Had sexier words ever been spoken?

I opened my mouth to reply, then snapped it shut. Had my brain left the building? Instead I shook my head and pointed to my throat.

He looked puzzled for a minute before comprehension dawned. "Laryngitis?"

I shook my head again and pulled out my notepad.

This was where things would get awkward.

I don't speak, I wrote then showed him the paper. I tried to avoid telling people that I was mute, as it was technically a personal choice.

He read it, then shrugged. "So, do you want to learn about drop spindle spinning?"

I nodded vigorously.

He spent the next ten minutes explaining how drop spindles worked, answering each of my gestured or written questions. I found the conversation remarkably fascinating, especially considering that it started with wool.

I was in the middle of trying to figure out how to casually ask for his phone number when a younger woman came up and tapped me on the shoulder. I turned.

"Hi, um, I'm sorry, but are you SartorialExperiment_4_6?"

I nodded.

She grinned and bounced on her toes. "I knew it! I'm so excited to meet you. I follow your TikTok and you are just so inspiring. I love love love watching a middle-aged woman taking up a new hobby!"

I tried not to wince. I was *not* middle-aged.

"I mean," she continued, "it's just so authentic and so raw, you know? Having these incredible adventures in learning to knit and do all this stuff from scratch! I love it!" This girl spoke in a *lot* of exclamation points.

I tried to smile. It was kind of sweet, how excited she was to meet me.

"Hey! Would you mind if we took a picture together?"

I shrugged.

She passed her phone to the drop spindle guy, wrapped her arms around me in a BFF-style hug, and posed.

I smiled in what I didn't think was too much of a grimace.

"So," she said, pulling back, "don't you just love these festivals? I love them! They're so inspiring!" She still bounced just a little.

I nodded.

About this time, she seemed to finally notice that I hadn't said anything.

"Are you from around here? Do you come to this festival a lot?"

I grabbed my paper and started writing again. She wrinkled her forehead in confusion and turned toward drop spindle guy.

"She's mute," he explained.

Her eyes grew wide. "That. Is. So. Inspiring!" She just about squealed. I could hear every bit of punctuation in her sentence.

She babbled for another minute or two, using at least thirteen more exclamation points. She was sweet, even if she should maybe lay off the caffeine, so I tried to act friendly in return. It wasn't her fault, after all, that I had never meshed well with the cheerleading crowd.

Finally she left, and I turned back to the drop spindle guy.

"Wow," he said. "That was a lot of enthusiasm."

I grinned and nodded.

"So you're some sort of TikTok celebrity then?"

I scoffed. Not even.

We chatted/wrote messages for another couple minutes before the next assortment of strangers arrived to ask questions and ogle the hot guy wielding a spindle. He introduced himself (Samuel), we exchanged phone numbers, and I left with a smile on my face and thoughts far more pleasant than the ones I'd been having in the months since the curse began.

For that reason alone, I was likely to fall in love with him.

I came home from the festival a muddle of thoughts and anxiety.

When was too soon to text? I didn't want to come off as desperate, but I didn't want to seem uninterested either. A casual text in a couple of days was probably right. Friendly but not too pushy.

To keep my mind off Samuel, I opened up my camera footage from the festival so I could make some TikToks. I clicked on one of the videos—Samuel juggling his spindle from hand to hand and laughing. I groaned. This was maybe not the best way to stop thinking about him.

Instead I opened my TikTok account to catch up on whatever messages I hadn't responded to.

I stared at the screen, frozen. Usually I heard from maybe one or two people per day. Not much, definitely not enough to get all the nettle contacts I needed.

But now I had twenty-seven messages. And another two came in while I gaped.

I flicked through the app and suddenly came across the photo of me and that girl from the festival. She had thirty-eight thousand followers. *Thirty-eight thousand.* She had *influence*. I watched her TikTok video in which she talked about meeting me at the festival and it was so cool seeing me in person and how I couldn't even talk and wasn't I so awesome and inspirational?

Yikes. I didn't want to be popular for something that wasn't even true.

I clicked back to my messages. Some were just fan messages, but there were also offers. People with fields that might have nettles. Suggestions for where to look. My heart started to pound. I pulled up my spreadsheet and added rows. More rows than I could have imagined a week ago.

I didn't like how it happened, but...

I needed this nettle.

So I swallowed the ick and started responding to messages. I hadn't been the one to say I was mute. I wasn't an inspirational story. I was just some random woman on the internet making really bad sweaters. It wasn't my fault that some of my followers were there for the wrong reasons.

At least that's what I told myself so I could do this thing. What else *could* I do?

I hadn't even finished going through all of the messages when my phone buzzed. Hardly anyone contacted me anymore, except via my TikTok (which was suddenly gaining attention, in the mysterious way of the internet, where people fall in love with cat videos and singing hot dogs).

I have a confession, the text began. It was from Samuel.

I stared at my phone, my heart pounding, my palms sweaty. A confession? That sounded promising. Well, unless it was a homicidal sort of confession, but he hadn't given off that vibe. I'd give him the benefit of the doubt. I clutched my phone tighter, hoping.

I thought about acting cool and casual, waiting a few days to contact you, but I'd rather just skip the pretending and get together again. Soon.

Butterflies erupted in my stomach. *Cool is overrated*, I texted back, also trying to sound cool. *Would love to get together too. Never knew drop spindles could be so fascinating.* *wink emoji*

I could tell you more, lots more. Lunch tomorrow?

Sounds good. *thumbs up emoji*

I spun in circles on my office chair, grinning like an idiot, my thoughts fluttering and memories of Samuel flying all around my head.

Outside, one of my brothers squawked.

Maybe being birdbrained was catching.

Samuel and I met up outside a little café near Lexington Market. He leaned casually against the aged brick wall, smiling at me with that delicious dimple. His jeans fit well, and he wore a button-down collared shirt—relaxed but nice. His hair curled adorably in the humidity, begging to be ruffled. And while we're at it, I might as well mention that his teeth sparkled and he would not have looked out of place on the cover of a romance novel.

He pushed away from the wall and came to meet me. "Hey there."

I smiled and waved.

He opened the door, and our date officially began. We "talked" through lunch, getting used to the give and take of me sending him texts while he replied out loud. It felt a little stilted at first, but it got easier. We talked through dessert too, and when his hand tentatively reached for mine across the table, I happily stopped texting and held on. I didn't think about nettles even once.

When our server started giving us dirty looks and pointedly wiping down tables nearby, Samuel stood with a sigh. "Can we do this again?" he asked.

I nodded enthusiastically. Some things didn't require words.

JUNE.
Fact: You don't have to be a prince to be charming.

Just like that, we were dating. Meeting for lunch or the traditional dinner and a movie. Walking through the Inner Harbor, watching the seagulls swoop and squawk. (I wondered if any of them were victims of an ES.) Touring the new art exhibit at the Walters and trying to make meaning from a series of sculptures that looked like giant potatoes. And, of course, practicing spinning. Thanks to his Sisyphean patience in teaching me, I was finally making progress with a spindle.

On a sultry June evening, we went on one of those touristy Fells Point ghost tours. The tour guide had just explained the grisly death of a sailor, along with his haunting of the local pub, and I was feeling twitchy. If witches were real, maybe ghosts were too. And what about werewolves, vampires, demons? I shuddered.

"You okay?" he asked, putting his arm around me.

I nodded, not about to explain the source of my thoughts. *Tell me more about your family*, I typed to get my mind focused on something else. He had one older sister who lived in the Midwest. His parents were happily married and had retired to Florida. No one had ever turned anyone else into a bird.

I, on the other hand, wasn't sure what to say when he asked about my family.

"You have any brothers or sisters?" he whispered to me as the tour guide described yet another brutal murder.

I nodded and held up six fingers.

His eyes widened. "Six? You close to them?"

I pulled out my phone. *They're kind of obnoxious sometimes, but I would do almost anything for them.*

"Do they live nearby?"

I thought of the coops on my porch (and the makeshift arrangements in my bathroom on cold nights) and nodded.

"It must be fun having family nearby," he said wistfully. "I don't see much of my sister or my parents. Do you like it?"

I shrugged and waved my hand in a so-so gesture.

"Do you ever get sick of them?"

I nodded. Then I nodded some more.

He chuckled. "Okay, okay, I get it. I guess I should be grateful for the space."

Yes.

He laughed again. I loved that sound. He asked how my spinning was going. I texted about it, carefully skirting my true purposes, treating my obsession like some sort of early mid-life crisis instead. He asked me about my TikTok, and I thought of the growing spreadsheet; I was finally starting to believe I might find all the nettle I needed, like a TikTok-influencing fairy godmother was watching out for me.

When he smiled, my whole body flushed until I could feel the blood pumping even in my toes. But I couldn't fall in love with Samuel. Not now. Everything was tainted by all the words I couldn't speak. I evaded his questions about how I'd lost my voice, looking away guiltily, and he didn't press it.

But when he looked at me and leaned in, none of the guilt mattered. All that mattered was closing that tiny distance between us.

I'd been kissed before. Not excessively—I wasn't that kind of girl—but there had been a few past boyfriends. A few casual smooches. That one memorable disaster that required a can of mace and a restraining order. And when I was alone with my TV and the remote control, I might occasionally rewind a movie to rewatch the kissing parts—not that I'd ever admit to it.

After *this* kiss, though, no Hollywood makeout scene would ever measure up again.

JULY/AUGUST/SEPTEMBER.
Fact: Sleep is overrated.

Harvest.
Date.
Smooch.
Rinse.
Repeat.

OCTOBER.
Fact: Torches and pitchforks aren't out of fashion; they've just moved online.

I woke to a glorious Saturday morning stretching out before me. Samuel and I had planned a picnic at Fort McHenry. I'd worked my fingers to the proverbial bone over the past two weeks, gathering all the local nettles I could find. They crowded the tiny backyard, flowed through my living room and upstairs to the bedroom, and filled the bathtub, where a few batches were soaking. I felt justified in taking a couple hours to spend with Samuel before I hunkered down for the marathon spinning/knitting event.

Besides, I planned to bring some gloves just in case we ran across a truly unexpected patch of nettles—who said you couldn't mix business and pleasure?

I rolled over and checked my email (before I'd gotten out of bed, just like any other normal person). My inbox was flooded. My TikTok notifications were insane. My blood pressure was rising.

"DIE, Horrable Lyiing Witch!!!!"

I stared at the subject line of the first email. Even ignoring the bad spelling, its meaning was a mystery.

The next was equally vicious, though more correctly spelled.

I scanned through the subject lines, and then through a few of the emails, marked by an overabundance of exclamation points, a variety of threats, and a surprising number of four-letter words.

My stomach sloshed.

Finally I went to TikTok, immediately finding the video that had started it all: a short clip from a family dinner a couple years back, one where I'd been laughing and singing (loudly and off-key) with all six of my brothers. A caption read, "I thought she was mute?"

I didn't even have to look at the name to guess who'd posted it. And yep, it was a user named ES_666. Well, that was appropriate.

I wanted to scream, then sob. I couldn't defend myself, not in words or in video. What could I even say? I hadn't meant to use my condition to garner support for my little project. I'd never played into it at all. But I'd also never denied that I couldn't talk. And I had gotten popular at least partially because of that girl so long ago who posted that fateful picture. The facts, from the outside at least, were damning—not that the internet ever needed a good reason to burn someone at the stake anyway.

Would Samuel hear about it? Of course he would. Would he still come? That was the question.

I dithered all morning, wanting to text him, too scared to do it, spinning my mind at least as much as I spun my threads, waiting in the silence to find out.

The doorbell rang a few minutes past noon, and I heaved a sigh of relief. He came.

My smile dropped when I saw his face.

"Can I come in? I think we need to talk."

I stepped back and gestured him inside. I'd done my best to hide at least a few of the mountains of nettle every time he came over, but it had gotten harder the longer we dated. Nettles in various stages of processing gathered against my furniture like snow drifts in a blizzard. Balls of yarn—both natural and synthetic—sat in mounds like they were waiting for tiny adorable dragons to claim their hoards. The disaster that had become my life could no longer be hidden.

In all the hours since I woke up, I still hadn't decided what I could say to him. Alien experiments stole my powers of speech? A little far-fetched. A deal with a crazy sea witch to exchange a voice for legs? That had already been done. A family curse? Too close to the truth. Nothing I said would explain it, and the one thing that *could* explain it I couldn't say.

All of this flitted through my mind again in the moments it took Samuel to pace into the room (admirably ignoring the nettle detritus) and turn to face me.

"I didn't think it mattered," he said, "and it still doesn't. Not really. Except that you've never explained how or why, and I don't understand." He blew out a breath. "And then there's this video, and you've got this beautiful voice, and I've never heard it."

I probably would have been touched that he found my voice beautiful, despite the terrible singing. You know, if it weren't for the whole liar liar pants on fire thing.

"Why?"

I couldn't meet his eyes, and mine felt wet. Good thing I hadn't put on mascara. I pulled out my phone to text him.

He grabbed my hand and stopped me. "Can you really not say it?"

I shook my head.

He let go of my hand to let me finish the message.

He wasn't going to like it.

He'd pulled out his phone too. This was the familiar rhythm we had; I'd type, he'd read and speak in response. When his phone chimed, he read.

I bit my lip.

I can't tell you. I wish I could.

I could almost see the words cross his mind. His jaw clenched, and he took a deep visible breath before he looked up again. "That's all you have to say?"

Please, wait until Thanksgiving, I pleaded. *Just believe me until then.* *hopeful face emoji*

"Why? Is it some stupid bet or something?"

I shook my head wildly.

"Then you're not making any sense. Why can you tell me on Thanksgiving but not now?"

Ugh. I wanted to scream, but of course I couldn't. I wanted to commit stepmatricide, but being in jail probably wouldn't help the relationship either.

Please just trust me. I promise I have a good reason. *annoying praying hands emoji*

He read my text and closed his eyes. A few moments passed, and I started hoping he might believe me.

Then he deliberately locked his phone and put it in his pocket. I couldn't tell him anything now.

Ouch.

I reached out to him, but he backed away.

Double ouch.

"I have to think about it." He stood there waiting for another minute, such hope and hurt in his eyes.

I looked away. I couldn't stand it. Just a little longer, not even two months, and then I could tell him. Then I'd try to explain. Then hopefully he wouldn't have me committed to an asylum.

Just a little longer.

When the door closed behind him, the floodgates opened and I bawled—silently, messily, snot and salt mingling on my blotchy face.

The virtual firestorm lasted three days and four cartons of cookies 'n' cream. Then some poor guy made the mistake of sharing a video of him teaching his kids to shoot BB guns at their old Barbie dolls. Soon the mob took their pitchforks and their anonymous comments off to his TikTok account. But for me, the damage was done.

Did I have enough nettle yet? My spreadsheet calculations suggested I was running short, and spreadsheets don't lie. I'd planned to ask for help from the last few contacts I hadn't used yet, but they'd all dried up. I was a social media pariah.

So I rethought the sweater sizing, reworking how thin I could make the yarn. The sweaters had to fit the human versions of my brothers, not the bird versions. Unfortunately, considering how much I fed them, their human forms had probably gained weight. I wasn't clear on the pigeon-to-human conversion calculations. But surely the sweaters could be muscle shirts, with bare midriffs and stubby sleeves, right?

I might still have enough nettle, if I was very careful, but that would take a lot more time in an already critical deliverable deadline.

Hey, on the plus side, my boss fired me—supposedly for some HR violation, but we both knew it was because of the social media pressure. I had zero income, zero future prospects, but a whole heaping lot of extra time.

Since I couldn't defend myself, I didn't even try. My spinning and knitting took on an air of desperation. Nothing mattered anymore but the sweaters. Not even that Samuel hadn't spoken to me at all since that day.

When thoughts of Samuel intruded, as they always did, I pushed them away. He wasn't *that* wonderful. So what if he had looked at me with a smoldering stare to rival Mr. Darcy (the Colin Firth version, of course)? Or that he had dreamy, hunky hands, also like Mr. Darcy (the Matthew Macfadyen one this time)? There must be hundreds of men out there who could manage that.

I blew my dripping nose and dried my leaking eyes. I could only lie to myself so much.

Even with all my extra time, by Halloween, I was still several shirts short. Time passed in a nettle-y fog and the mounds of fibers shrank bit by bit. Every day was pretty much the same: bingeing Netflix, twisting mountains of fluff into yarn, knitting the skeins of yarn into rows and rows of lumpy sweater, caught up in the mind-numbing boredom of counting garter stitches and stockinette (was it my imagination, or did knitting sound like lingerie?). My fingers flew like my life depended on it.

Which was technically not true.

It was my brothers' lives on the line.

I hated to imagine what life would be like for them, or for me, if I failed. Pigeons forever? Not even the most obnoxious, most crazy-making brothers deserved that. The thought only added to my sweater-filled nightmares and frenzy.

I was running out of time.

NOVEMBER. Thanksgiving, to be exact. Again.
Fact: The more things change, the more they stay the same.

My head snapped up from the couch back, and I looked toward the clock, my heart racing. I hadn't meant to fall asleep, but my eyes had drooped beyond my power to keep them open. You could only consume so much caffeine before sleep deprivation caught up to you.

I had half an hour left. I breathed a sigh of relief; at least I hadn't overslept the deadline. On the other hand—or wing—my last sweater was still one sleeve short, and I didn't have time to finish it. I glanced back and forth between the clock and the sweater. Maybe I could whip out a couple rows and that would be enough. After all, who really knew what counted as a sleeve?

There was a knock at the door. I looked up, panicked. What now?

I wanted to ignore the knock, but it came again, louder and more insistent, and the doorbell rang too. A tiny part of me remembered asking Samuel to wait until Thanksgiving. Maybe, just maybe, he'd come back? A thrill ran through me, and I raced to the door.

A man in a uniform stood on the porch. I slumped. Stupid hope. "Kelly McPherson?"

I nodded.

"I have a warrant here to search your premises for illegal pigeons."

This couldn't be happening. I was so close. Another hour and I wouldn't have any pigeons at all. This reeked of the ES.

I would not let her win.

I reluctantly let the man in. I'd filled out the paperwork to keep all my stupid pigeon brothers, though I'd fudged a little bit about where I'd "purchased" them. It was absolutely legal... if only I could find my copy of the permit. I had definitely put it somewhere that seemed smart at the time.

I explained this quickly on a little whiteboard I kept by the front door. Surely I could find it and get him out of here in record time.

"I've also been told their living conditions are unacceptable."

I rolled my eyes. I would hazard a guess that their human living conditions had been more unacceptable than their pigeon living conditions. It was practically the lap of pigeon luxury these days, especially since the recent cold snap had made me bring them to live inside again. They'd always been wimpy about cold weather.

I looked at the clock. Time was ticking. I wasn't going to get any more knitting done. I had no idea where my pigeon permit was. It was now or never.

I pointed him outside to look around the backyard.

I closed and locked the door behind him with a quiet click.

I snatched the five completed sweaters sitting beside the couch and the sixth sweater, with just the left sleeve missing. My heart raced faster yet.

I dashed up the stairs toward my brothers' bathroom home, and behind me I heard the back door rattle. Muffled yelling issued from behind the glass. I hoped I could convince him later that the door had just gotten stuck. But for now I couldn't think about that.

I raced into the bathroom and let the pigeons out of their cage. One by one, I tossed the sweaters over their heads and held my breath.

It started out slowly, a small hissing sound, like the air being let out of a tire. Except instead of deflating, the pigeons did the opposite. They... expanded. Like hair mousse sprayed from a can, swelling larger and larger until I realized I should move out of the bathroom to give them some room.

With a final hiss and a tiny pop, there they stood before me. One moment pigeons, a few moments later, brothers.

I turned away faster than you could say "Egad, no!"

Brothers wearing nothing but sweaters.

Nothing.

After a few minutes of hasty confusion involving towels and blankets wrapped around waists, I suddenly remembered the animal control officer. Crap.

I rushed to the back door and hastily unlocked it.

The man was not pleased.

I picked up my whiteboard again, then realized I didn't have to use it. "Sorry, that door is sticky," I croaked. Apparently a year of not speaking turns you into a frog. Better than a pigeon. "Must have closed by accident."

He looked at me funny. "Why'd you write everything on that board before?"

"Ummm... I've been... sick. Yeah, just trying to rest my voice after having laryngitis." I turned my pleading eyes on him. Maybe my feigned illness would butter him up.

He glared at me. Apparently the sympathy angle didn't work. Instead, he stomped past me to investigate the rest of the house. I sagged against the wall and sighed in relief. He wasn't going to find a single illegal pigeon. I didn't even care that wandering my house was probably outside his legal rights.

Plus, I enjoyed the idea of his shock at finding six pantless men hanging out in my spare room.

Several minutes later, the officer returned, looking decidedly uncomfortable. He told me I'd been warned and they'd be keeping an eye out to make sure I wasn't illegally harboring any pigeons without permits. I nodded, trying to keep my expression serious, then politely shuffled him out of my house.

I went back to the spare room and this time gave all six of my brothers a proper hug. Well, Joseph ended up with a feathery left arm (stupid missing sleeve), so that wasn't exactly a proper hug, but it was close enough.

They were back. I cried with relief. It was over, and I had won. Mostly, anyway (sorry, Joseph).

We all stood around awkwardly, not knowing what to do next. James bobbed his head, clawed at the floor with his bare foot, and mumbled his thanks. Jack tried to scratch his armpit with his nose. Being human again was going to take some adjustment.

There were a few more mumbles of gratitude, then Jared went to the fridge to rummage. At least some things hadn't changed.

I plopped on my couch, leaning my head back to stare around my surprisingly empty living room—no more drifts of nettle yarn, no more mounds of carded fibers. Curse ended. Marathon over. There were still brothers flitting around the house in the background, but everything else was different.

I didn't even have to think about the next step: I was going to win Samuel back.

I imagined it would involve a lot of explaining, and I hoped it didn't end with a restraining order, but I had to try. I fished my phone out of my pocket to text him, pleading with him to come see me. I had explanations to make. The sorts of explanations one could only make in person, especially if one didn't want to get hung up on.

Then I waited for a response.

And waited.

And waited.

I sank farther into the couch, deflated. I was not going to burst into tears again. That was useless and just made my nose run. I was going to be sensible and work on Samuel Recovery Plan B.

My tear ducts weren't listening.

Well, I amended, grabbing a tissue from a side table, I wasn't going to cry for very long. Just a little cry, and then I'd get to work. I deserved it, after all. I'd knitted all night, broken a curse, and seen my brothers without pants. Surely I'd been the hero enough for a couple of hours.

I heard Joseph calling a pizza place to order several large meat-lovers. They would probably eat all my Chinese takeout leftovers, too, but I didn't care. I curled up in a ball on my couch, ignoring everything. Samuel had not texted back.

"Yo, Sis," Joseph hollered from the living room. "Can we borrow some cash to pay the delivery guy?" I rolled my eyes. Count on brothers to pull a girl out of her wallowing. I wiped my nose, straightened my shirt, and went to find my purse.

A few minutes later, the doorbell rang. I grabbed my cash to pay for the pizza, then threw open the door.

It wasn't pizza.

Samuel stood there, looking at me. I stared back, a glowing smile spreading across my face. *He came.* Nothing else mattered. The corners of his lips looked like they were trying not to turn into a smile in response. Oh, how I'd missed that dimple. Much better than pizza.

I opened my mouth to find the words, but he started talking. "Look, Kelly," he said. "I don't know what's going on with you. I tried to just forget you, but I couldn't stop thinking about how you told me to wait until Thanksgiving. Then out of the blue you text me today, so here I am. I tried to talk myself out of it and move on, but I couldn't." He ran his fingers through his hair and sighed. "I think I love you. And I want to trust you. I don't understand, but you said you had an explanation. I'm here for it."

My heart wanted to burst. It would be okay. I reached out to him.

He wrapped his arms around me. I closed my eyes and sighed. It felt so good. I was in his arms. He'd come back.

After a minute, I drew in a deep breath. This was it, the moment that could make or break things. I pulled back so I could look into his eyes when I spoke. "Thank you," I croaked. My voice was midway between frog and princess.

His eyes went wide, and he sucked in a breath. His arms loosened, but they didn't let go. "Wh—what? You can still speak?"

I nodded.

"But why? Why would you fake it all this time?"

I took his hand. Such a familiar gesture that filled me with warmth. "It's a long story, and I've been dying to tell you." I pulled him toward the living room, where the twins joked about plucking Joseph to make pigeon pie. I rolled my eyes. "But first, let me introduce you to my brothers."

The Elf and the Fisherman

ONCE UPON A TIME, there lived an elf by the seashore. Now, it is a little-known fact that elves love nothing more than the pleasure of making shoes.

Sandals, slippers, boots, brogues, clogs, latchets, heels. If it fits on the foot, with or without a stocking, an elf would be happy to make it.

At least, most of them would.

This elf, however, did not like to make just any footwear. He was determined to make only the best. The best of the best, in fact, a pair of shoes fit for a king. Nothing else would do.

Each day he would sit in his workshop and fashion his shoes. The cool sea breeze washed through the open windows as he worked, but he did not notice. A bird sang sweetly in the tree outside his shop, but he did not care. His soul was intent upon one thing only: to make the perfect pair of shoes.

Each day, as he came to the end of his task, he would examine his workmanship. Yes, he thought to himself. This stitching is very fine. He smoothed his hand across the tooled leather toe box or the soft sheepskin lining. Supple, he thought, nodding with pleasure. But then—and this happened every day—a flaw. One stitch a little too long. One scuff across the heel. One shoe bearing a set of markings barely a shade off from its match. Not a single set of shoes was perfect.

He would huff to himself, disgusted with his day's work, and storm outside with the shoes carelessly dangling from his hand.

The sunset before him, spreading out across the ocean, blazed a fiery red, with a flash of green. The world seemed set aflame for an instant, but he could not be bothered to see its beauty. He walked to the edge of a small cliff that bordered the ocean, and with an arm strong from his cobbler's work, he would throw each shoe as far as he could into the sea.

He turned in disgust and went back inside to sleep, dreaming of the next day's work.

Now, it just so happened that in that same land, there lived an old fisherman.

He had weathered many a storm, spent years on the ocean pulling in his catch. His dearest dream, the one he kept closest to his heart, was to fish from the ocean the greatest fish anyone had ever caught. He would do it someday, he told the other townspeople. And when he did, his fame and riches would abound.

So each day he went out to sea, catching fish after fish, waiting for the one that would make him happy. But it never came.

Then one day something strange occurred. He was sitting in his little boat out on the ocean, his pole before him, his line sliding invisibly into the depths, when he felt a tug. Now, this was nothing new, but it was a strong tug, and he hoped that finally this day he would catch the fish of his dreams. He reeled as quickly as he could, and at last, he pulled his catch over the side.

A boot.

A finely made, if a little damp, men's boot.

He shrugged and tossed it into the back of his boat. *I will deal with it later*, he thought to himself, and returned to his fishing.

Another few minutes and another tug brought him the second boot of the matching pair. This was indeed odd. But fishermen are used to mystery. The sea holds more things than any land folk could ever appreciate, and this man had seen more than most. So again he tossed the boot into his boat and continued to fish. However, the boots turned out to be the final catch of the night, and it was time to return home.

He was greeted at the door that night, as he had been every night for thirty years, with a kiss and a smile from his wife. When he held out the boots and explained their appearance, she took them with the composure of a fisherman's wife. She quirked her head to the side, dried them off a bit, and placed them in the closet. Neither of them thought any more of the boots that night.

The next day was as fine a day for fishing as any the man had ever known, and he eagerly set out in his boat.

That day the man caught two pairs of shoes: a lovely set of ladies' slippers and a handsome low-heeled shoe for wearing in fine weather. He shrugged as he brought up each shoe and tossed them into the back of his boat. Then he went back to fishing, still determined to catch that one perfect fish. When he returned with the four shoes, his wife kissed him, shrugged with him, and again dropped the shoes into the closet.

This went on for many days, each day yielding a catch of several pairs of shoes. By now the man and his wife were growing quite a collection. They tumbled out of the closet and into the front room. Small mounds of shoes began to form larger mounds as the footwear piled up. And still, every day, the man went out in search of the fish that would make his fortune.

Finally, the man returned home one day with his catch to find that his wife was not there. He rushed inside to look for her, fearing the worst, searching frantically through each room of their home. A sound from behind him made him turn, and there she was, panting and out of breath. She had been on an errand in the village and had run all the way back to try to return home before he did.

She explained to him what she had been doing, and slowly the man began to smile.

The next day when the man left his home and headed toward the docks, the little old woman left as well. She headed in the opposite direction and carried a small crate of shoes under her arm. All day long, as the man fished, the woman carried. Back and forth, back and forth, and slowly the mountains of shoes diminished to hills, the hills to mounds, until finally there was nothing left.

When the man returned home that night, his wife gave him his usual kiss. And then, beaming, she dropped a coin into his hand. Their very first sale. They had opened a shoe store.

In time, their shop became famed throughout the country for the quality of their shoes. Eventually even the king heard of them and sent for his very own pair. The elf's gorgeous creations were worn by a king. The man's catches brought him fame and fortune. And the man and the woman never wanted for riches again.

Diamonds and Pearls

It was supposed to be a gift.

But she hadn't spoken for five years now, so obviously it was a curse.

She remembered that summer day in Central Park. She'd stopped for a moment to guzzle water from her bottle in the ninety-degree shade.

"Spare a drink for a stranger?" asked a weak voice from a few feet away. Anne looked toward the voice's owner, a small woman in ratty clothing, dirtier than the ground beneath her. Then she looked dubiously at her water bottle, imagining the swarms of bacteria on the woman's lips.

But it was hot, and the woman was old. The least she could do was help. So Anne gave her the bottle and watched her drink greedily.

Passing the bottle back to Anne, the woman wiped her mouth with her sleeve and said in a voice somehow both stronger and lighter, "Thank you. You are kind indeed. For this kindness I shall bestow upon you a marvelous gift."

"You don't really need to—"

The old woman swept to her feet, suddenly radiating power as she held up her hand for silence. "This is your gift: The words that fall from your lips shall fall in jewels."

Anne gaped in horror. She reached out in supplication, but the sun broke through the trees, momentarily blinding her. When she could see again, the woman had vanished. She cupped her hands to her mouth. "Please no," she whispered, and two small objects dropped from her lips.

A ruby. An emerald.

She knew how this would work in a fairy tale, of course. A handsome prince would ride up on a white horse and declare his everlasting devotion. He would carry her off into the sunset to live happily ever after.

But this was not a fairy tale, and in her world a woman whose words produced jewels could never be safe—not from science or the press, not even from a prince who might declare his love. She would never be sure of anyone's true intentions. She would never know whom to trust.

So she stopped talking. Her voice became a rusty memory. Even a cough creaked like an unoiled hinge. The words she would not speak began, instead, to pour out of her onto paper. Her passions, her fears, her hopes, her dreams—they spilled from her like blood, saturating the pages with her life. Pages became chapters became novels became bestsellers. Money flowed into Anne's bank accounts. In her nightmares, it flowed in sapphires and garnets, opals and amethysts.

She hid inside her books. She used signing when required, but her refuge was a profound silence in which both her lips and her hands were still.

Then she met Daniel. Kind, funny, smart, handsome. Everything she'd always wanted. As the cold winter sun warmed to spring light, she felt the tightness within her begin to relax. She began to hope. And fear. She plucked petals from a daisy in her heart: *He loves me. He loves my money. He loves me.* And no matter which petal dropped last, the daisy always fell to the floor with the same question: *But what if he knew about the curse?*

It could not go on forever, she realized. So as spring edged toward the brightness of summer, she decided she would no longer live imprisoned by her cursed gift. "I have something to tell you," she signed to him, unable to meet his eyes. They sat together on the very bench the old woman had occupied so long ago.

"I do too," he said, smiling.

She gestured toward him. *You first.*

He took her hands, his eyes warm and bright. "I love you, Anne. I want to marry you."

Her heart sped as a smile rose unbidden to her lips. How she had longed for this, prayed for it. Maybe his love would be strong enough to keep her secret safe. She shook with the hope of it.

She took a shuddering breath and opened her mouth to form forsaken words. "I love you too." Her voice creaked from disuse, and his eyes widened in surprise. They widened even farther as she put her hand to her mouth and spit.

Tiny objects glittered in the sun, lustrous and pure as true love in the fairy tales. She held them out for him to see: diamonds and pearls.

She raised her eyes to meet his. The love in them was brighter than jewels.

Forged in Iron and Blood

Lina had left the war long behind her. That's what she told herself, anyway. Especially on nights like this when dusk fell through the open doors of the smithy and the fire blazed in the forge and in her blood. But the crash of her hammer against the metal was too like the clamor of battle, and the memories kept flooding back.

The pulse of the fight, the tang of blood in the air. Friends bleeding and dying, both fae and human, their lifeless bodies strewn across the field. Such pointless, wretched loss. She swung the hammer again, hoping to drive out the pain and forget herself in the work. To forget their naivety—*her* naivety—in believing that peace could come so easily. The oathbinding magic was certainly rare and powerful. But no promise made to one foolish half-blood fairy could end the simmering tension between the two countries as quickly as it ended the actual battles. If only she'd—

"Lina-smith," a bright voice called from the doorway.

Lina shook herself from the memories and turned around, a practiced smile covering her thoughts. "Seelah," she greeted with false cheer. "How are you this evening? How's the newest grandchild?"

"Delightful, of course," Seelah said, beaming as she bustled in. She dropped her basket on a table and eased herself onto a stool. "Oh, but don't let me stop you"—she gestured for Lina to keep working—"I'm just here to have a little rest."

Lina chuckled to herself and stoked the fire again, enjoying the distraction; a "little rest" meant Seelah had gossip to share.

"You'll never guess what I heard today," Seelah began, pausing to speak between the clangs of Lina's hammer. "Jinnel was arguing with her husband—well, you know that's nothing new—but she brought up her great-aunt, and she threatened to head off there and stay with her for good. And then he…"

Lina let the stream of words wash over her, Seelah's voice a soothing reminder of the peace that Lina had fought and killed and sacrificed to protect.

"…So I thought I would drop by some soup tomorrow and just check in on her. Would you care to join me?"

Lina snapped out of her thoughts again. "Oh, um, yes. Always glad to lend a hand," she replied. "Come by tomorrow at dusk?"

Seelah agreed but lingered, waiting.

In answer to the unspoken question, Lina smiled wanly. "I'd invite you over tonight for tea, but I'm exhausted. It's straight to bed for me." She looked toward the open doors. "Must be the cold weather coming, always makes me sleepy."

Seelah picked up her basket to go. "Another time, then. I do enjoy our chats by the fire."

"I do too," Lina said, and she meant it.

Maybe it was time to move on, though. She'd been living in Solime for years, getting too comfortable in her role, playing the friendly grandmother maybe a little too well. She was bound to accidentally reveal something true about herself, make a mistake she couldn't afford.

Or maybe she was just getting old; her hair was more gray than black now, and though smithing had kept her strong, it was getting harder to creak out of bed in the mornings. Maybe it was just natural that she was restless and thought more about the war these days, as she was drawing near to leaving everything behind for good. She'd played her part for as long as she could, but she couldn't avoid the end forever.

Lina stepped back from the forge and surveyed her smithy—a few small worktables, stacks and buckets of scrap metal, projects and tools hanging from the ceiling and lining the walls. A good place. A place to forget and be forgotten.

She stripped the heavy leather gloves from her fingers and stretched her hands, easing their tired muscles and massaging the scars that crossed her palms. She'd amassed more burns and cuts than she could count. She rolled her shoulders to release the strain of hours bent over her work. A cold breeze blew in through the doors, and she welcomed the chill. She was right—the weather was cooling. There would be snow soon.

She raked the coals from the fire, set them to cooling, and made sure her tools were put away for the night. With everything in its place, Lina closed the shutters over her window and took one of her smaller hammers down from the wall; being a blacksmith meant that no one thought it odd for her to walk around with weaponry. She latched the door shut, dropping a small nail in the dirt so it leaned carelessly against the door. The actions had become automatic, almost meaningless, but there was comfort in the familiar.

The path home was short, her little cottage nestled in the space just behind the smithy. As she approached, she slowed and eyed her surroundings. Nothing disturbed. A particular pebble lying on her porch was in the same spot as usual. She stepped over it, slipped inside, and set her hammer by the front door.

She twitched her rug to the side, checking that the entrance to her hidden room was undisturbed, and glanced toward the brick in the hearth that covered a store of coins. Everything was in its place. She could rest, banish the clash of weapons still echoing in her mind. For now at least. She closed her eyes and listened to the stillness with a smile. Tomorrow, maybe, she'd think about moving on.

Lina startled awake, her eyes wide and staring, her heart pounding. She'd been dreaming, of course—of Mollen. Her dearest friend, her brother-in-arms, her once-upon-a-time hope for the future. In her dream, she watched him fight, just as she had so many times in life. He was grace and beauty, the swing of the sword, all dance and brilliance. Watching him, it was easy to forget, for the moment, the devastation of war.

Then the sunlight had flashed against the torque around his neck, and the dream became a nightmare, a memory.

But that wasn't what woke her now, in the gray hours before dawn. There had been a noise. She listened, her body tense.

Then she heard it again. Outside and very near. A grunt of pain. A sound almost as familiar as ringing iron.

She pulled on her overdress, picked up her hammer, and crept out to investigate, every sense alive to danger. Though dawn was near, the space behind her smithy was swallowed in darkness. Lina listened again, raising the hammer, as her eyes darted from shadow to shadow.

In one of the deeper shadows, Lina saw it. Something, anyway. A huddled form, large enough to be a grown adult, curled up against the wall where the heat from the forge warmed the bricks. It didn't move. It didn't belong.

Maybe this would be the moment when danger finally caught up with her. Maybe she would find out if she could still fight. Her blood pumped with vigor, her heart answering the possibility for battle. She stole forward.

A whimper and a few muttered words emerged from under what she could now see was a torn, stained cloak. "Hurts... stop... can't..."

The voice was deep enough to be male, though human or fae she didn't know.

Lina breathed deeply once for calm. "Hello?"

He writhed and moaned but didn't respond. Lina peered more closely, almost feeling the waves of panic rolling off him. She adjusted her grip on the hammer's wooden handle. His face was hidden, and he wrapped his arms protectively around himself under the cloak. She studied him, warrior and grandmother battling inside her. She could help him. It could be a trick. She should protect him. She should watch her back.

After a moment of indecision, the grandmother took over. She crouched and set her hammer beside her. If anything was amiss, there was always the dagger concealed in her skirts.

"I'm going to help you," she whispered soothingly, the way she would talk to a terrified child. She got a hand under his arm, pulling him to his feet. He was frail, lighter than she'd expected, even as he leaned heavily on her, one hand now reaching up to rub against his neck. She shuffled him forward, bearing most of his weight and still scanning for danger, until they reached her cottage.

With a bit of maneuvering—and a brief, regretful glance at her clean blanket—Lina settled the man in a heap on her bed. She locked the door and checked that her window shutters were tightly closed, then started a hearth fire going. She kept one eye on the stranger.

Now that he was stretched out in the glow of her fire, she had her first clear view of his clothing and cloak, both of fine wool but ragged beyond hope of repair. His hair, a dirty brown, hung lank and tangled, and he had maybe a week's growth of beard. Whatever he was running from, he'd been running awhile.

He started to mumble again, tears slowly streaking his face. "Need help... Can't think... Hide." He reached his arms toward her, then yanked them back and tugged his tattered cloak more tightly around his neck. "No." He convulsed. "Yes." He shook his head.

The pain tugged at her, and she forced herself to ignore the tightness in her throat at his suffering. *Focus on what you can do, focus on solvable problems,* she thought. So she fetched a cup of water and dipped a cool cloth into it. She brushed the cloth across his forehead and his bright red cheeks as she looked him over. No obvious external wounds, but by the way he alternately rubbed at his neck, then tugged his cloak more tightly around him, something must be wrong with his neck. He groaned when she moved his head and batted at her hands when she reached for the clasp of his cloak. She stifled a sigh at his resistance, then pushed his hands away and yanked at the two sides of the cloak.

It tore apart, revealing the man's neck. And around the man's neck, a familiar metal torque—an echo of her nightmares—caught the glow of the firelight.

She leaped to her feet and drew her hidden dagger, her joints protesting at the speed of her movement.

The war *had* come back to her, in a way she'd tried to never think of again.

Her muscles tensed, and her heart raced as she crouched in a fighting stance, waiting for him to pounce. He didn't look like a warrior—in fact, he looked more than half dead. But she had no idea the extent of the torque's powers. For all she knew, it could make even the half dead fight like dragons.

"Please," he muttered. "Help me." He opened glassy eyes and looked up at her, pleading, clawing at his neck like an animal caught in a trap. "Don't"—he shook his head slowly—"don't let them have me."

"Who? Why are you here?" A thought suddenly struck her with a wave of horror. "Do you know who I am? Were you here for me?"

But he had lapsed into unconsciousness, and no matter how she nudged at him—dagger at the ready—he only tossed feverishly.

She fetched some cord from a cupboard and bound him quickly to the bed, then backed away to a safer distance, where she could observe the man and think. She *had* to think, ignore emotion, ignore the queasy wash of sadness and anger and fear that lapped through her.

If someone was making these torques, something dangerous was on the horizon. Of course, it couldn't be war again, not with the oathbound pact still in place. The rulers of both lands had sworn in carefully worded oaths that there would be no war between their countries, and that pact would have to be honored as long as the oathbinder lived. But even without causing outright war, the torque could make plenty of mischief.

Or maybe it had nothing to do with the tension between the two lands, but whatever it was, it had to be stopped.

As she settled onto the edge of her kitchen chair, her eyes were drawn to the torque again. It caught the firelight and flickered almost like a living thing. Where an opening should be, allowing the wearer to remove the torque from around the neck, there was only smooth metal. She couldn't look away, and she couldn't stop the memories that she'd tried to hide from for so many years.

The only other time she'd seen an object like this had been during the war, when Mollen had disappeared for two weeks, then suddenly come back, changed. They'd thought he was captured by the enemy while on a secret mission, so when he returned, she'd rejoiced and rushed to greet him. He didn't even glance her way. She'd taken him to report to the commanding officers, hiding her pain at his treatment. Other soldiers had gathered to hear where he'd been. He'd stood in front of them all, and then, without any warning beyond one short cry of pain, he'd thrust his sword through the commander and started cutting down his fellow soldiers. His movements were jerky, not his usual perfect grace—almost like a separate battle raged within him. A strange metal torque around his neck shone in the sunlight as he moved.

The torque the stranger wore was the same. She examined it carefully. The skin around his neck was red and raw, and when she touched it, he moaned. She swallowed and closed her eyes against the man's suffering, but that only took her back to Mollen. She had watched in shock for a moment; then she and several other soldiers had flown into action, striking at him with shocked rage. A part of her detached itself then, unwilling to feel the agony of that battle. Within minutes, he was dead, and Lina was numbly thankful that someone else had struck the fatal blow. She didn't know if she could have survived killing him.

After Mollen's death, several fae spellworkers—only the fae had magic, of course, and only a few truly understood how it worked—had studied the torque. It had been imbued with mind-turning, a magic forbidden, and largely forgotten, for centuries. Mollen's treachery was not his fault. Someone had broken his will, turned his mind, and sent him back as an assassin.

Now someone was using this magic again. The knowledge seared through her. Mollen. She'd tried so hard to forget him and the pain of his death. She'd turned that pain to good, to helping stop the war once and for all. Or at least for a long while, hopefully long enough for real peace to settle in. She'd sought—and found—her own measure of that peace.

But seeing that torque again... Rage burned within her, brilliant yellow and malleable like iron in the forge, waiting to be shaped to her purpose. Someone had dared to experiment with such brutal magic again, and it could not be tolerated. *She* could not tolerate it.

Lina crept back to the smithy to gather her tools and returned to her still-unconscious visitor.

She examined his neck and the torque again, then placed clamps on its edges and began to tighten them. Tricky work to remove the cursed item without killing the man beneath; she might have given up if she hadn't known what it was. She gritted her teeth and continued applying pressure.

Finally, with a satisfying snap, the torque broke and fell to the dirt floor. The man breathed in sharply, then rolled to his side. He opened his eyes, glassy and unfocused. "Thank you," he whispered, then he closed his eyes and took a deep breath.

"Who did this?" Lina asked, desperate now for answers. He didn't respond. She nudged him, gently at first, but with increasing strength. "Where are they?" she asked, shaking him now.

Still no response. It was as if removing the torque had released him from life and pain. She watched helplessly as his breathing slowed, becoming gentler, softer, until it dwindled to nothing.

She leaned back, sighing. The yellow burning inside her dulled under the weight of death, and she swiped at her eyes.

She straightened his hands to his sides, swallowing to relax the shaking of her own hands. "From dust to dust," she murmured over the body, speaking the human last rites. "From breath to tears." She'd said these words over so many others, she hardly had to think about it. She paused, then added the fae blessing for good measure—more words she knew by heart. "Full circle, like the moon. Full season, like the earth. Rest now, beneath them both." He didn't look fae, but she knew very well there were plenty of mixed-bloods who could pass for human. The burning of iron on fae skin was the only foolproof way to tell, and since she hadn't tried it on the poor tormented man, she'd never know if he was part blood. The iron test didn't work on the dead.

She closed her eyes for a moment of stillness. Fae or human, she wished him peace.

But the moment couldn't last. What if he *had* been there for her? Did they know where and who she was?

Probably not. Solime was a busy town despite its size, with people coming through all the time. It was likely just the wildest of luck that he had happened upon Lina.

Still, she'd be careful. It was definitely time to leave, one way or another. Just as soon as she'd dealt with things here.

She couldn't ask anyone to come to her aid. The local watch weren't equipped to deal with powerful magic, and the only other help was too far away. When the war had finally ended with the oath-bound pact, Lina had disappeared. All but one of her old contacts thought her dead, and she meant to keep it that way. As soon as she could, though, she'd write to that one contact, her "sister" in Hillfar. Her sister would inform those who still watched for such dangers, they would hunt down whoever had created this torque… and Lina would disappear again.

But that was a job for later in the day. No one would arrive in time to help her with her more immediate problems: a body in her house, the torque on her hands, and no idea who was coming or how long it would take them to get here.

She peeked out her shutters. Muddy light was brightening by the minute, and soon the whole town would wake. She picked up the torque and stared at it with loathing. It was beautiful, if you didn't know what it was for. The carvings were delicate, in an old fae script. Lina knew little of the metal used to make it—she'd not been a smith that first time long ago, and the gleaming silvery material was far too rich, too rare, too difficult to work for a lowly blacksmith. The magic too.

Who had made this new torque? None of the fae she'd known during the war could have done it, and anyone who'd been able to had been executed.

She'd thought.

She wrapped the torque in a tea towel and placed it in the pocket of her dress. All her thoughts turned to one purpose: to destroy it.

Heat it to the upper limits of her forge's ability so it would melt down to liquid, then mix the metal with so much iron and impurity that it would be unrecognizable. Cool it back into a lump of scrap and bury it where it would never be found.

She left her house, noting the pebble's location with more care than usual, and scurried to her smithy, formulating a plan. She'd destroy the torque as quickly as possible, and if they came looking before she had a chance to disappear, she'd play the innocent, ever-so-helpful grandmother. She smiled grimly as she lit and stoked the fire, imagining her part.

She drew the torque from her pocket and stared at it again, revulsion and fascination intertwined. Some people said that mindturning was a bit like oathbinding. Both were magical interference with a person's will, after all. With a simple promise, a person was absolutely bound to carry out their words. With a powerful and careful enough promise, like the pact that ended the war, the course of history could change. Two sovereigns of two lands had sworn to cease fighting and do all they could to ensure peace—and for years they had. Some believed a mindturn could do just as much good.

She shuddered as she thought of Mollen. Those people were wrong. Some oathbinding, it was true, involved a bit of trickery, but it could never take from someone more than they were willing to speak. The monarchs who had promised to stop fighting had done so of their own accord. Their people were tired and hurting. They hadn't been forced into magical enslavement. An object of mindturning destroyed a person's will and deserved, in turn, to be destroyed.

The fire was almost hot enough now—a little longer and then she could do it.

A knock at the door interrupted her. Startled, she shoved the wrapped torque into a bucket of scrap iron beside her and kicked the bucket to the side as Seelah pushed her way into the room.

"Good morning, Lina!" she cried, dropping that ever-present basket on Lina's counter as usual and launching into a story about a neighbor down the road who had lost a goat and wasn't that a shame and what could have happened to it and that reminded her of the new strangers in town who had arrived just recently and how they looked rich and—

Lina often thought that as a source of information, Seelah would have been infinitely useful in the war. As a keeper of secrets, though, she would have ruined everything.

Suddenly one detail of Seelah's words stood out. "Did you say strangers?" Lina interrupted.

"Oh yes. I mean, of course there are always strangers, but these men seemed... you know... somehow different." She leaned forward. "Powerful. Rich." She smiled. "Maybe they'll need a new sword, or one of their horses will throw a shoe. You might get some business."

But Lina wasn't listening—now was not the time to start a long round of gossip. She picked up Seelah's basket, pushed it into her arms, and started nudging her toward the door.

Just as three men stepped into the doorway.

The first was richly dressed and short—she'd imagined whoever came would be tall—and had the fine features that often betrayed a bit of fae blood. Interesting. The others followed behind him like servants as he strode casually into the room. Lina wasn't fooled. They strolled, but their muscles were tense. The one to the right kept his hand near his sword, and the short one prowled like a cat preparing to pounce. There would be no new sword or thrown shoe to deal with, just the torque and the dead man.

Lina kept her eyes from wandering to where she'd hidden the torque, but her mind began to spin. This was going to make things much more difficult. She cursed herself for her stupidity. She'd been so slow, too slow.

"Greetings," she said, her voice friendly. "I'll be with you in a moment." For now she just needed to get Seelah out of danger. She continued to push her friend toward the door. "Thank you so much for stopping by," she said. "It was nice to see you, and I'll come visit you later, *just like we planned.*" She wanted to establish, in front of these men, that she'd be missed if she disappeared.

Seelah gave her a hard look, glancing quickly between Lina and the men. "Yes," she said slowly. "Yes, just like we planned. I'll expect to see you in... an hour or two."

Lina nodded. "Have a lovely day!" she chirped, pushing Seelah out the door and shutting it behind her.

She'd known Seelah would remember their plan to meet and deliver soup today, but that was later in the evening. Why did Seelah say they'd meet so soon? Whatever the reason, Lina shrugged and set it aside. It worked better this way—now the men knew that if she disappeared, she'd be missed very, very soon.

She turned back to face them. "Good day to you."

The short one nodded in return. "And to you." He'd been looking around the smithy, and while his glance suggested a casual appraisal, the sharpness of his eyes missed little.

"What may I do for you this fine day?" she asked.

He moved away from the wall of tools he'd been scrutinizing, his appraising stare on her now.

She continued to smile. How could she salvage her plan? In her imagination, the torque was safely destroyed before they came for it, not sitting in a bucket of scrap metal a few feet away.

"My name is Tyblith," the man said. "I'm looking for a friend. I've been taking care of him, but he ran away. He's terribly sick, you see. He gets confused. Ends up thinking I'm his enemy and runs off." He shook his head, all sorrow and worry and honest innocence, but he watched her closely. "Have you seen him?"

Lina's thoughts flitted. Part of her said to trust him, he was so honest and thoughtful and—she mentally shook herself. What was she thinking?

No, she couldn't trust him, and she had to come up with a plan. Now. "Oh! I'm so glad you've come," she said breathlessly. "I've been wondering what to do. He's sleeping in my house, but he was afraid to let anyone know where he was. He's been so very distraught and feverish—well, you know that, of course. I just didn't know what to do! But now that you're here, I'm sure he'll be happy to see a friend." She finished and drew a breath, ready to start babbling again if necessary.

"You found him, then?" the man asked sharply.

"He's in my home, just behind the smithy. You can all go see him and—"

"Maresk, Toren, look for him. I'll stay here and talk with this"—he turned a charming smile on Lina, his voice softening—"this lovely lady here."

"Oh, I don't mind if you all go check on him. He's probably resting anyway."

"No, my men will be able to take care of him. I'd much rather you tell me how he appeared at your home."

Tyblith nodded at the other men, and they swiftly left.

Blood of the nix, he was staying with her. She'd hoped they might all go together and she could still throw the torque on the fire in the minutes they were gone. Time for a different plan. Again.

"Oh, the poor man! He just showed up last night and collapsed!" She clutched at her chest. "I took him in, of course. Nothing else I could do, poor creature. He reminded me of my dear aunt Milla, when she came down with the—"

Tyblith interrupted, already bored by her narrative. "Did he... say anything?"

"Well, not—"

The other men burst back into the shop. "It wasn't there," one of them said abruptly. "And he's dead."

"Dead?" She gasped. "No, he couldn't be! I just left him less than an hour ago, and he was only sleeping." She wrung her hands. "Oh, so cruel. Fever sickness is terrible."

Tyblith glared at Lina. "Did he say anything to you? Give you anything? Tell me!"

She cringed, looking back and forth between the three men. She reached over and took a large iron chisel down from her wall, holding it out in front of her awkwardly, as if she hoped to use it to protect herself but had no idea how. Hopefully, it made her look afraid and also reminded them that she couldn't be fae. "I don't know what you mean... I was just trying to help him. Don't hurt me." She made her voice tremble in fear, even as her blood pumped with anticipation.

He sighed and rubbed his hand across his forehead, his whole demeanor softening back into his original charm. "I'm sorry," he said, the note in his voice turning pleading. "I didn't mean to alarm you. I'm just so stricken by his death. He was my good friend, you know."

The shift in his emotion was so abrupt, Lina almost swayed toward him, longing to comfort him in his grief. So he was a charm-speaker, then. Her earlier desire to trust him made sense now.

"Yes, I can see that," she replied, and she, too, softened her voice. She lowered the chisel. "I'm so sorry for your loss. You must have been close."

He frowned. "Yes. I'll miss him. And he was in my care, so I feel responsible for him. His mother will be devastated."

Lina nodded. "Poor woman."

"He had a gift from her. He wore it all the time, even though it chafed awfully." He stared at her as he spoke his next words. "It was a torque."

Lina widened her eyes. "A gift from his mother, you say? Someone he *loved*?"

Maresk and Toren seemed to shift uneasily, but Tyblith only hesitated for a moment. "Yes." She could almost see his thoughts flying. "But... they'd been fighting. Yes, they'd been fighting, and he was very angry at her. So you can see even more why she'll be so upset. I was just hoping to comfort her, let her know he had it with him to the end."

Lina visibly relaxed the tension from her shoulders—they noticed it, of course—and smiled. "Oh, that explains it!" She tittered. "He was babbling on and on about how I needed to destroy it right then and not let anyone have it or do anything bad with it." She shook her head. "He was probably just being spiteful, hmmm? Didn't want her to know that he'd forgiven her and was still wearing it. People do silly things when they're fighting, don't they?" She tsked, shaking her head.

"So you have it, then?" he asked, leaning toward her in his eagerness.

"Of course I have it. Honestly, I'm a little relieved to give it to someone else to take care of." She paused—this was the most dangerous moment—and looked into Tyblith's eyes. "Can I trust you?"

He exuded honesty, almost like a scent. "Of course you can."

Lina leaned in and whispered, "Look, I just don't know what to do. This poor sick young man showed up at my home, and of course I took him in. But then he started ranting and wailing, and he made me swear I would help him and that I had to keep the torque away from the wrong people. Now, I'm not the kind of person who breaks promises." She paused, looking at him with concern.

"No, of course you wouldn't do that," he said, but his eyes darted around the room, looking hungrily for where the torque might be.

She shook her head. "No, I wouldn't." Her voice took on a desperate edge. "You're telling me it was a gift from his mother, but how can

I know? I promised him the torque wouldn't be used for ill. That's all he seemed to care about." She forced a quiver into her lip, then bit it to stop the tremble. "And now he's dead, and that makes it his dying wish, and of course I have to do what I can to help him, and here I am just a tired old woman." She tugged his sleeve with the hand not holding the chisel. "You understand, don't you? Why I don't know what to do with it or who to trust?"

He patted her hand and spoke soothingly. "Of course I understand. Such things are so difficult. But I can assure you I was his friend." He looked into her eyes, sincerity in his every feature. "You can give me the torque," he said. "You don't have to worry anymore." She felt his charm fall over her like a warm blanket, soothing, telling her to believe.

She blinked, breathing deeply. *Focus on your purpose,* she thought. *Focus on Mollen and the torque.* Her mind stayed clear. "But are you the right person? He was so worried something bad would be done with it." *Come,* she thought, *say what I need you to say.*

"If you give it to me, nothing bad will be done with it." His voice was so smooth, his charmspeaking so very easy to believe.

She blinked again, straining against the magic. "You promise?" she wheedled. "No one will use this torque for anything bad?" She nearly held her breath.

He opened his mouth to speak, then paused.

Maybe she'd gone too far.

His eyes flicked to the chisel and her bare hand wrapped around it. She could almost see his thoughts. *This old woman is a simple blacksmith. A promise to her is meaningless.* "Of course I promise," he assured her, all friendliness and honesty.

Lina blew out a breath and smiled her first real smile since they'd come. "Oh, I feel so much better. I know it's crazy, but thank you for humoring a poor old woman."

He shrugged. "Of course, dear lady. Nothing to it. The only thing that torque is good for is comforting another woman like yourself, after all." He held out his hand.

She stepped to the bucket and fished out the torque. "I'm just glad to be rid of it."

He snatched the metal from her and examined it.

"I'm sorry it's broken." Then, as if she'd just thought of it: "I could fix it for you if you'd like!" It might give her a chance to come up with a better plan than this; she still hated seeing that object in his hands.

He shook his head, not looking up from the metal. "No matter, I have a friend who can fix it."

She nodded. This would have to be good enough, then.

They should be going now, but Tyblith didn't move. He just placed the torque in a pouch at his side and turned his eyes on Lina. Maresk and Toren glanced at him, waiting, muscles tensing beneath their tunics. A nearly imperceptible difference in the air had Lina tensing too. Moments passed, and she shifted her weight to prepare for an attack. Part of her hoped they would try something, despite how foolhardy it would be to attack the town blacksmith in her shop in daylight. The idea of letting them leave with that torque—no matter what she'd done to keep them from using it—stoked the anger again. Maybe it was good she still held the chisel.

Tyblith turned to the side, gesturing to his men. Lina took a steadying breath.

"Lina!" a familiar voice cried as the smithy doors swung open. All four bodies swiveled toward the noise. Seelah burst through the doors, an even larger basket in her arms this time. That woman had so many baskets. She looked back and forth between the men and Lina. "I'm so sorry to interrupt. I forgot you were in the middle of something. I'm just so overcome!" She blinked rapidly. "I've received a messenger from Innalue in Hillfar. You know, the one who's friends with *your sister*. There's been a terrible accident, and she's asked for us at once."

Lina could only blink and stare, yanked out of her preparation for battle. She didn't *have* a sister in Hillfar—how could this Innalue woman be friends with her? What, by the nix, was Seelah doing?

Seelah leaned toward the men, explaining in an undertone, "I'm her best friend, and I must have Lina's help, so you see we simply must go. Immediately." She paused and looked piercingly at Lina. "You're needed there, Lina. Everyone will be expecting you."

Lina blinked again, then shook herself from her stupor. She had no idea what Seelah was playing at, but she would go along with it. "Well, good sirs, I'm so sorry, but it looks like I'm needed at once. I'm sorry about your friend too. Do give my best to his mother for me."

A moment passed, then the men sprang back to life. "Yes, thank you, Lina-smith; we will," Tyblith said. "May we retrieve his body from your home?"

"Of course. I'll come with you." After they left, she could get to her hidden bags and leave Solime. Seelah had given her the perfect excuse.

The men left the smithy ahead of her, and when Seelah stepped out, Lina dropped the chisel into her pocket with a quiet hiss. She'd have to examine the damage to her palm later, when she was alone. For now, she curled her fingers softly around the bright, angry burn marks.

The entire group headed to Lina's house, and the men quickly picked up the body and hauled it out to the cart they'd left in front of her smithy. Tyblith turned back once to stare at Lina standing in her doorway for a moment—then at Seelah—before nodding and disappearing down the road.

Would she ever hear of them again or know what became of the torque? She hoped not. Better that they, and their plans, fade quietly into obscurity.

When the sound of horse hooves had faded, Lina breathed a sigh of relief and focused her gaze on Seelah.

"Do be quick with your bags," Seelah chided. "I'd rather be gone from here in case they decide to come back." She shivered. "I'll get the one in the hearth, but you'd better get that one." She pointed toward the underground room. "I don't think I can get up and down any ladder you've got down there."

Lina's mind reeled. "How did you—?"

"Come now, I've known about your hidey holes for ages. You really need to stop glancing at them during tea." She shook her head in mock reproach.

Lina's mouth dropped open for an instant, then she began to laugh. "All these years—I've underestimated you, Seelah."

Seelah shrugged. "Just because I like the town gossip doesn't mean I don't know when to keep my mouth shut."

Lina shook her head in wonder. Apparently, Lina was not the only woman in town who was not what she seemed.

The two of them worked swiftly to gather what little Lina wanted to take with her—and of course her hidden stores. They put most in her pack and the rest in Seelah's basket.

"Now, I don't know exactly what's going on here, but I'm going with you to Hillfar, or at least far enough to be sure you're safe. You can tell me all about it, or not, as you please."

Lina nodded. It would be good to have someone else with her in case Tyblith and his men decided to follow her. Or in case they found a way around the hurried oathbinding she'd set him to. If they were smart, they might realize that the irresistible desire to be done with that torque had come directly after Lina had convinced Tyblith to make that promise.

And if they realized she was responsible for that, they might wonder if Lina was the one who'd bound the pact to end the war. And then she'd be running, hard and fast. There were people who would like to exact revenge on the one who'd helped create the peace. A few, most of all, who would like to kill the oathbinder to release the magic of the pact.

She glanced down at her hand again, at the red blisters seared across older, faded lines. All the times she'd held iron and pretended that it didn't burn. All the ways she'd hidden in plain sight—who would suspect a blacksmith of having fae blood? She looked at Seelah. She'd done it alone for so long, but she really was getting older. It might be good to have a friend who knew the truth, who could help her if the war followed her again.

As it always did. It was always in her heart, burning in her blood like iron. But she would create all the peace she could, as long as she lived.

She turned to Seelah as they left the house. "What do you know about the end of the war?" she asked. She didn't reset the pebble.

The Nanny Job

"Oh, for the love of Peter Pan," Snow White muttered. Not again. She rushed over to the food stand where Rosie was looking pathetically up at the vendor, begging for whatever treats he sold. Snow glanced at the placard: The Magic BeanMobile. She hadn't seen this one before, but the park's food vendors rotated frequently.

Snow grabbed Rosie just before she reached for a vanilla bean ice cream cone. "I told you, no dessert until after our picnic."

Rosie pouted.

Standing next to her, her sister Goldie smirked.

Snow turned on Goldie. "Don't think I didn't see you begging too. And don't go telling me nothing at breakfast was just right and you're so starving."

Now Goldie pouted.

Snow took a breath before she turned on her most sugary voice. "Off to the playground, young ladies. And don't get in any trouble." She shooed them toward the slides and turned back to the vendor. He was tall with dark hair, dark eyes, and the hint of a smile. "Sorry she tried to con you," she said.

He shrugged. "No problem." The side of his mouth twitched upward, revealing a dimple. She'd always been fond of dimples.

"I haven't seen your cart here before. Are you new?" she asked, casually tossing her hair. That generally had a pleasing effect on men.

He grinned wider, and she found herself distracted by the discovery of a second, matching dimple. "Yup. Had a recent windfall, decided to follow my dream—and here I am, running my own culinary empire." He gestured grandly at the modest cart. "Would you care to sample my vanilla bean ice cream?" he asked, proffering a cone.

She blanched, but then all those self-defense classes kicked in. In an instant, she'd pulled her can of mace from a hidden pocket and brandished it at him. "You stay away from me," she hissed, veins pulsing with adrenaline.

He held up his hands, one of them holding the cone, and stepped back, eyes wide. "No problem. It was just a friendly offer."

She blinked, frozen for a moment, then suddenly realized people were staring. Snow took a trembling breath and shook her head, trying to shake loose the terror. "You're right, I'm sorry. I... I *really* don't like gifts."

He nodded, his hands still up. "Noted."

Snow grimaced and inwardly sighed. Well, that was the end of that flirtation. She looked down, muttered another apology, and walked over to the playground, trying to forget the unfortunate little run-in. Only three hours until she handed the girls over to their parents.

Nannying had seemed like such a good idea when she'd started it. It was just a trial run, after all—three months while the girls were on summer break before second grade. Nothing she couldn't handle, and maybe she'd finally found a solid career path.

Because it hadn't been her first idea.

She'd tried quite the assortment of money-making techniques before she came to this place. Beauty pageants first, because her high school and college classmates had voted her hottest girl in school. The pageants were easy, but winning got boring after a while. Then she'd tried jewelry making, hoping all the time she'd spent around miners would give her skills (it didn't). Next came maid service jobs, since she'd done that sort of thing before—and nothing, she'd thought, could be more disgusting than an eternal bachelor pad filled with seven men who worked in dirt all day.

She'd thought wrong.

After that, she'd applied pretty much anywhere she thought she could get a job. It had been an arduous (and not terribly lucrative) couple of years.

Finally, after a bit of soul-searching and some really expensive therapy, she decided to try nannying. She liked taking care of people, she was friendly and well-educated. She'd developed some common sense, and she would never again take apples from strangers.

Which is how she'd ended up watching the annoyingly precocious Locke children.

She snapped out of the memories and looked at the girls, who were now whispering conspiratorially. That couldn't be good.

Maybe she was being paranoid. They really weren't that bad, not all the time. It was just that they were always egging each other on—the double-dog-dares, the constant "bet you can't do this." It inevitably ended in trouble. If only they channeled that energy into something useful like schoolwork, athletics, baking for their granny.

Snow sighed and pulled a self-help book from her purse: *Your Mother Was a Witch*. The current chapter was "You May Have Trust Issues." No kidding. Magic BeanMobile guy and the ice cream kerfuffle was just the latest in a series of related mishaps.

Like the time she'd tried out Kismet, the latest dating app, and met this guy who'd seemed perfectly charming. Until the day he gave her a box of chocolates. She made him eat half of every single one in case they were poisoned. Looking back, that was probably the beginning of the end of that relationship.

Snow turned the page then glanced up to check on the girls. It had only been a few paragraphs, but Goldie was gone.

She ran to Rosie. "You are going to tell me exactly where Goldie went," Snow said through gritted teeth. "Or so help me, no desserts for a month."

Rosie shrugged. "I'll just go beg some for Grandma." That ploy always worked.

"Fine," Snow said, panic rising. She looked around the playground, her eyes darting from slides to grass to nearby trees. Where would Goldie have run? Surely not the trees? Hadn't she learned her lesson last time, with those bears?

Probably not.

Snow took Rosie's hand and began to drag her toward the trees.

"This is yours, isn't it?" a voice behind her said.

Snow glanced back to see the Magic BeanMobile guy, holding tightly to the wrist of a squirming Goldie.

Snow nodded, resigned. Maybe the Lockes would fire her for losing Goldie, and she wouldn't have to think of an excuse to quit yet another job.

"What was she doing?" she asked with a groan.

He grinned. "Stealing some edamame."

"Did she break anything?" she asked in a rush. "Eat any other food sitting out? Are you pressing charges?"

He shook his head, extending the arm holding Goldie. "Nah."

Snow accepted Goldie's wrist. Goldie just pouted and wouldn't meet Snow's eyes.

Snow looked back at the food guy. Well, this was awkward.

"I'm sorry," she blurted. "I swear I didn't put her up to it as some sort of weird revenge. I'm their nanny, and I really was paying attention to them, I just—"

He held up his hand to stop her. "No need to explain. I'd only turned to get some change when she sneaked in. She's a speedy one. Quiet too." He nodded, almost impressed. "Bright criminal future ahead of her, that one."

Snow let out a startled laugh. "You have no idea," she said with a smile. "I'm sorry she bothered you though." She glared at Goldie, in case she'd forgotten that she'd misbehaved.

Goldie grumbled. "I knew we could pay for them."

He chuckled, and Snow was distracted by those dimples again.

"No harm done." His voice turned stern as he tried to scowl at Goldie. "But don't let it happen again."

Goldie rolled her eyes.

"I'm Jack, by the way." He held out his hand to Snow, and she took it.

"Snow."

"Nice to meet you, without the mace and all."

She cringed. "Thanks for not calling the cops. Twice."

"No problem... Maybe I'll see you again sometime."

He hadn't been scared off yet by all this craziness? Wow. When he grinned this time, her heart gave a little flutter.

The next morning she suggested a jaunt to the park. It seemed like the right day for it. And maybe they'd stop and try a new food stand. For fun. Maybe the girls would be in the mood for chili or edamame or burritos.

None of this had anything to do with a certain handsome, heart-fluttering BeanMobile owner.

She had done her makeup perfectly, dressed in her cutest top, and worn her favorite skinny jeans. This was also pure coincidence.

When they got to the park, she casually perched herself on the bench nearest the food stands then pretended to be fully absorbed in watching the girls play. Come to think of it, they were behaving remarkably well.

Suspicious.

She didn't have time to analyze, however. "Hey, Snow!" Jack's voice called from behind her.

She turned and smiled in fake surprise. "Oh! I forgot you worked here."

"Yep, same as yesterday."

She definitely hadn't fooled him. Oh well, hard-to-get was overrated.

He beckoned her over. "Want to come chat? You can still see the hoodlums from here."

"Welllll," she said, "I suppose I can do that."

Two hours, three bean enchiladas, and not a single act of Goldie-and-Rosie mischief later, Jack and Snow had arranged to get together the next week.

If she primped a little longer for this date than she ever had for a date with any of those dating app dreamboats, what of it?

That's how it all started, and now they'd been dating for almost a year.

She still nannied the girls, but since it was the school year, she only had them a couple hours a day, so she'd stuck with it after all. They never complained that they constantly ended up at the park, and she never had to chase them down again. Sure, they giggled and nudged each other when they saw Jack, but she'd gotten used to that. Plus, they'd kind of grown on her.

For her birthday, Jack had pointedly *not* gotten Snow any presents. Same for Christmas and Valentine's Day. Though, he told her, he did think she would have enjoyed his collection of Fabergé eggs. But she was still dealing with some baggage, so it seemed safest for them both if he kept his gifts to himself.

Until one spring afternoon at the park. Jack had been busy selling black bean burgers, cocoa bean puddings, and refried bean tostadas while Snow White made eyes at him and watched the girls.

But then, suddenly, Jack stepped away from his cart and took something from his pocket. A little black box.

Snow's eyes widened with surprise.

Jack knelt in front of her and held out the box.

Snow vaguely heard the gasps of various bystanders, but all she could see was Jack.

"I know you don't like gifts, but I'm hoping, just this once, you'll accept this one from me." He opened the box. "Marry me?"

She looked from Jack to the ring and back again, waiting for panic to flood her. But none came. Her heart raced, true, but only in excitement. A slow smile spread across her face, and she nodded.

Jack jumped up and swept her into his arms. Snow laughed happily. This was really a therapeutic breakthrough. She wanted to tell him. She wanted—

"Ha! I did it!" Goldie's voice broke into Snow's thoughts.

Snow and Jack pulled apart to stare at the girls.

Rosie rolled her eyes. "Only 'cause I let you!"

Snow wrinkled her brow, confused. "What?"

Goldie giggled. "I got you and Jack together. Rosie dared me to."

"And I didn't mess it up 'cause he's so cute," Rosie said, grinning. "Although I could've if I'd wanted to," she muttered under her breath.

"But you didn't get us together," Snow said.

Goldie rolled her eyes. "Course I did! Why else would I steal the edamame?"

Because you're a juvenile delinquent, Snow thought. "For fun?" she said aloud.

"Duh! To make you talk to Jack! Begging the ice cream didn't work—and then we didn't even get to eat it." She pouted.

Snow blinked. Was it true?

"I thought you should date this flute player guy we met," Rosie added, "but we found out he was a major creeper and he liked rats." She shuddered.

Goldie nodded. "I'm good at figuring out what's just right for someone. *Way* better than Rosie is. I knew you'd like Jack."

Snow's thoughts whirled. Had this really all started with a dare?

Beside her, Jack began to laugh. "Girls, you are evil geniuses." He smiled, dazzlingly.

Mmmm, those dimples.

Finally Snow just shrugged and turned back to kiss Jack. Who was she to argue with a happily ever after?

Daughters of Sea

I HAVE BEEN A daughter of the sea, my tail flashing as I slide through the water.

I have been a child of earth, dancing upon two feet through steps that felt like knives.

I have been, for mere moments out of eternity, almost nothing—just a bit of brine and sea foam.

And now I am a spirit of air, lithe upon the wind, tossed about on invisible currents. No body but a puff of air, no tail, no feet, no brine.

In the sea, I was innocent, naive, but free. On the earth I suffered, but oh the exquisite joy of that pain. In the wind I am witness to all the world at once, its beauty and its misery. I exhale, I nudge, and the world changes. Amazing what a gust of wind can do. And yet, I can only observe, I experience nothing for myself.

I no longer know where I belong. The question passes through me, rustling through my thoughts like the current through the seagrass. Where is my soul meant to be? For I have, I am told, finally earned that soul.

It is a question I cannot answer, though I have asked it often in my three hundred years of wind.

My time here is over. I can feel a shift in the breeze, though not its direction. Perhaps I finally will disappear, from air to brine forever despite that promise of immortality. Perhaps I will return to earth or sea. Or perhaps, I think to myself, I will rise up from the wind into fire, one final element. Perhaps I will rage into storm, a bolt of lightning crashing down through the air, over the sea, striking a ship made by men of the earth. Perhaps I will set the ship afire in a great burst of power, and the cycle will be complete.

Will there be, far below me in the water, another child of the sea to rescue the human flotsam of my destruction?

Some Restrictions Apply

SAMRIN WAS A YOUNG man, a trader by profession. He traveled from village to village, buying and selling cloth, pots, trinkets. His dreams were few, as he was a happy man who needed little to be content.

As he walked one day along the dusty paths between villages, he kept his face down to avoid the glare from the afternoon sun. Suddenly in front of him, he saw something glinting in the dust. It was a lamp, dirty from the road, but otherwise in good condition.

Interesting, he thought. *Maybe I can trade it for something.*

So he picked up the lamp and rubbed it on his shirt to clean it. No sooner had he done so than a mysterious smoke billowed from the lamp. The smoke formed itself into the shape of a man. Samrin had heard tales of such men—genies, twelve feet tall with bright blue skin, admiring fans, and the ability to create full-scale Broadway musical productions with the snap of a finger. He'd never believed them before, as the tales tended to be shared in pubs after several mugs of drink.

But here was a genie, undeniably in front of him. Yes, the genie was more purple than blue, and certainly not twelve feet tall. But what did such minor details matter?

The genie stroked his goatee with an air of great importance. "Who dares to rub my lamp?" his voice boomed, loud and deep. He placed his hands on his hips and posed magnificently.

"Me, Samrin," Samrin squeaked. He shivered in fear and asked, "And who are you?"

"I am the great genie Erequat," the genie boomed again. "Since you are the possessor of my lamp, you are now entitled to three wishes." Then, in a much smaller voice that Samrin barely heard, he muttered, "Some restrictions apply."

"What was that?"

"Oh, nothing," Erequat said. "Now what is your wish? Remember to choose wisely."

Samrin thought for a few moments. Despite his general contentedness, there is always something that can be improved upon.

He had often been plagued by allergies, and he had a spot that was always sore in his left arm from a nasty pastry kneading accident. Wouldn't it be wonderful to be rid of those? "I would like to be perfectly healthy for the rest of my life," he declared.

Erequat scratched his head. "Hmmm... That's a problem." His voice got a little whispery again. "You can't wish for anything that directly affects your person. It's against protocol, you see. We'd have people all over the place asking for perfect beauty, immortality, all sorts of ridiculousness. So, no blue hair, no long eyelashes, and no perfect health." Suddenly he returned to his booming voice. "You must try something else! Be careful what you wish for."

Samrin thought again. Life on the road was good but sometimes lonely. "How about a beautiful woman to marry and love all my life?"

"Oh, no, we can't have that." Erequat shook his head sadly. "The rules strictly forbid influencing someone else's ability to make their own decisions."

Samrin was a reasonable fellow and realized that was fair. He wouldn't want a woman who only loved him because of magic anyway. So he thought some more. "I know," he said, certain he had a good wish this time. "A big pile of money." After all, money did make life easier.

Erequat looked distinctly uncomfortable. "Are you, by chance, familiar with the laws of thermodynamics?"

Samrin stared, blank-faced.

"You see, I'd like to, but it turns out that you can't create stuff out of nothing. No big piles of money from thin air." He shrugged apologetically.

"Well, can you just take money from somewhere else? Or how about some jewels or gold or something?"

"*Steal?* You want me to *steal?*" Erequat looked appalled.

Samrin backpedaled. "No, never mind, of course not." He continued to suggest various wishes—nice weather for his vacation, a good deal in his trades today, maybe an extra tasty dinner?—and for each wish, Erequat shook his head.

Finally, fed up, Samrin threw his hands in the air. "Never mind, I don't want any wish at all."

Erequat's booming voice was back. "Who dares to rub my lamp but not receive his wishes?"

Samrin blinked. It didn't seem like a good idea to anger a genie, no matter how powerless the genie seemed. He cast his eyes around for an idea.

On the ground near his feet were three plain stones, each about the size of a fist. He pointed. "How about those stones? Can I have those?"

Erequat muttered to himself about rules, restrictions, requirements... After a moment, he boomed out, "Yes!" He picked them up and handed them to Samrin. "And for your next wish?"

Samrin shook his head vigorously. "Oh no, I'm sure there must be a rule about how many items I can receive per wish. I'm sure each stone takes up one wish, so I'm all done." He was backing away now, hoping to get far, far away from Erequat before he came up with any other ridiculous rules or restrictions.

Erequat nodded. "Yes, you're probably right. Yes…" He drew himself up proudly again. "Be thankful for this day, tiny mortal, the day you met the great and powerful Erequat."

Samrin plastered a pained smile on his face. "Yes, of course. Thank you ever so much."

Erequat turned back to smoke and sucked back into his lamp, waiting for the next lucky traveler to make a wish. Samrin tossed the rocks aside and hurried on his way, content once again but much less likely to pick up trash on the side of the road.

Song and Storm

GRAN AND GRANDPA MET by the ocean and fell in love like magic; that's the story they always told. Gran would sit on the porch swing and squeeze Grandpa's hand as they talked about those days, and her eyes would glaze over as she looked far into the past.

He was wearing a silly floppy hat, she'd tell me, strolling along the beach like all the other tourists in town on a lazy summer break. But suddenly the wind gusted and tore the hat off his head. It blew and flew and came to a stop at her feet.

Gran was sitting on a rock, humming to herself and staring out to sea.

When the hat stopped beside her, she knew it was fate. She picked it up and settled it on her own head. "You want this back?" she asked him, batting her eyelashes.

"Depends," he said. "Do you come with it?"

Gran laughed at his ridiculous response, and in that moment their lives were changed forever. "He found me irresistible," she used to say.

"Well, not *quite* irresistible." He would add this with a small smile, and their eyes would sparkle at some inside joke.

They had married within the year and settled down and built a little cottage so they could walk beside the ocean every day.

Every summer of my childhood, Mom and I spent a month with Gran and Grandpa in that cottage. "For the peace of the ocean,"

Mom would say. But also because she could sleep in late, let Gran cook breakfast and make fancy smoothies, and stop being the mom for a while and just be a daughter again.

Those summers, I splashed in the water, walked through the sand, collected hundreds of seashells, and glued them together into sculptures. At night I fell asleep to the crashing of waves and the cries of seagulls. We played, we relaxed, and I heard their story and basked in their love.

Then there was the summer I was eleven. It's been nearly forty years, but I will never forget. I was lying in bed one night, restless, staring at the ceiling with this nagging feeling that I was missing something. I rolled over to try to get comfortable and might have fallen back asleep, except I heard a creak and a hushed giggle as someone tiptoed past my room. A moment later, the front door quietly opened and closed.

I couldn't bear the idea that the grown-ups were doing something fun without me, there in the middle of the night.

So I slunk across the wooden floorboards of the house, dodging every creak. I'd made a game of it a couple of years before, learning exactly where to step so I wouldn't make a sound. I slid out the front door and followed two sets of footprints in the sand down to the beach.

The walk was short, and I hid behind rocks and shrubs along the way. The last hiding spot before the open beach was the lovely black boulder that still sits outside the cottage, the perfect place to sit and watch the sun set.

I crept behind the boulder and peeked over its edge. There were Gran and Grandpa, running barefoot toward the water, holding hands, still giggling. As they came closer to the water, Grandpa slowed down, and Gran went on ahead until she reached the waves. She stepped into the ocean slowly, raising her arms toward the sky. Then she began to sing.

It was the strangest song, wild and bittersweet and full of wanting. I'd never heard Gran sing like that before. Her voice was normally soft and leathery, the way I thought a grandma should sound. But this was... unearthly. I wanted to rush into the waves to listen. Only the fear of punishment kept me in my place.

She continued to sing, and Grandpa walked toward her until his feet were in the ocean too. The water began to swirl around them in unnatural eddies and swells, sparkling in the moonlight. Faster it went, and I watched in stunned silence as it rose higher, pushing the ocean away, leaving the sand beneath their feet dry.

All I could do was watch as the ocean spun and Gran sang and the whole world shifted.

Gran... had magic.

Gran had *magic*!

What else could it be? She sang, and the ocean obeyed. I wanted to obey too. I think I felt it even then, though I didn't understand it—the constant tug of magic, the urge to come closer, draw back.

When the spell finally released me, it felt like waking from a dream. Head spinning, I ran back to my bed, still hearing that eerie song echoing across the waves.

I slept late the next morning, and when I finally woke, it was to a raging fever. Gran took one look at me and set to fussing, cooking her homemade chicken broth and distracting me with silly stories that barely made sense to my fevered brain.

Summer vacation ended four days later. I spent three of them sleeping, lying around listlessly, and watching Gran, eager to learn more of her secrets. And every day she cooked and cleaned and pampered, so utterly *normal*, and as my fever abated, I began to wonder if I'd imagined it all. Maybe my illness had set in earlier than I'd realized, and it had all been a feverish dream. Magic wasn't real, after all, no matter how much I might wish it were.

The rest of that year, I tried to put it out of my head. Summers were a different world from regular life. I'd been ridiculous, I'd been sick, I'd hallucinated the whole thing. The more time that passed, the more unbelievable that night seemed. I turned twelve that winter, and I was too grown up to believe in magic. By the time summer came again, I'd mostly convinced myself I had imagined it all. And when Gran came bustling through her front door and down her porch steps to greet us, I knew: No one could be this ordinary and otherworldly at the same time.

"Hello, my loves," she cried, putting her arms around me and holding me tight, then reaching out and pulling Mom into the hug too. "I've missed you." She looked down at me. "Oh dear, look at you, so lovely and tall."

"Like those weedy bits between the rocks—tiny today, huge tomorrow," Grandpa said. "But don't smother them. Let the ladies come in for some air conditioning."

Gran rolled her eyes. "As long as you fetch their luggage." She took our hands, and her grip was softer than last year as we walked inside. The exertion of her greeting seemed to have winded her.

Mom cast a worried glanced at Gran. "You okay, Mom?" she asked.

Gran smiled. "Of course I am, sweetie. Just getting a little old."

Mom frowned, and the worry stayed.

That summer sped by, and while Gran seemed tired, everything else was the same. She took care of us, bought too many presents, fed me too much sugar. Grandpa grilled the world's best steaks, and Gran roasted corn on the cob.

They laughed as they worked, brushing fingertips and exchanging smiles. And as the sun set, Gran turned on the oldies music, and they shuffle-danced on the back porch in the evening breeze, pulling me and Mom into the dance while Sinatra crooned and Armstrong trumpeted and the whole world seemed right.

Did I watch her more closely that summer? Of course I did. Even while I told myself that I wasn't watching her at all and that I definitely didn't believe in magic, I still hoped a little.

She never sang, never even hummed, even when the house was filled with music. I asked her about it, but she only laughed and said, "Trust me, no one wants to hear this singing voice."

I tried to sleep lightly so I could listen and follow if I heard those footsteps outside my door. But I was growing, and I was exhausted from full days of sun, sand, and ocean. The few nights I managed to stay awake, the hallway floorboards were silent, everyone exactly where they were supposed to be.

By the end of the summer, I was fully convinced. I had made it all up. Gran's only magic was these beautiful, uncomplicated, perfect summers, suspended in time, each day glossy and brilliant and carefree. Nothing more. But that was okay, I told myself as Mom and I said our goodbyes and loaded our souvenirs into our run-down sedan and drove away. It wasn't as exciting as real magic, but there was a quiet comfort in it.

That comfort lasted, warm and soft, through the first days of school, through fall, right up through the first storms of winter.

Until I met Matthew.

Matthew moved into town halfway through the school year. He seemed so nice at first, smiling, introducing himself, wanting to make new friends. And because he was something fresh and different, we all wanted him to like us. There was a collective rush to claim the new kid for ourselves.

But it wasn't long before I saw how his laughter always had a victim. He found the things people felt worst about and picked and prodded until they lashed out. Then he looked astonished that anyone would blame him for the outburst.

I was little. I was shy. I felt powerless. I could only watch it happen, even when he turned his cruelty on me. Even when he asked with such oily friendliness why Dad didn't show up at parent night or the holiday concert or the cookie exchange. Lots of parents couldn't make it to those things; it shouldn't have been a big deal. But he knew somehow that it was, and once he'd found a weak spot, he wouldn't let go.

It hurt, yes, but hurt turned to anger. Days and weeks passed, and the tide of that anger built as I watched him humiliate the people who couldn't fight back.

Maybe I would have been fine, maybe I could have contained it if he hadn't started on my best friend Sara. Or at least, that's what I sometimes tell myself, but I doubt it was true. Eventually, I still would have reached a breaking point.

It came one February day after school. The snow was just shy of slush—miserable to walk in, wet, and dreary. Dad was meant to pick me up if the weather got bad, but I knew he'd forget. I gave up before I'd waited even five minutes. I zipped up my coat, preparing for the slog.

I'd crossed the street, heading toward home, when for some reason I turned to look back at the school. Sara was there, and Matthew, and a few other kids who followed him around. I couldn't hear anything except the laughter. But I saw the way Sara shrank into herself, trying to disappear.

I wanted to go back, confront him somehow, but I was scared he would turn on me next. So I stood, in cowardice, as Sara's eyes filled with tears.

My helplessness overwhelmed me then, washing over me and sucking me away from myself in its riptide. Until suddenly, a voice in my head whispered over the waves, *No*. I did not have to let him do this. I could stop him. I didn't know how, but I knew I could.

I opened my mouth. At first I whispered it: "No." Like the voice in my mind. A tiny, useless breeze of a word, disappearing almost as soon as it was spoken. But then I spoke again, louder, with more conviction. "*No.*"

The words themselves meant nothing, but each time I spoke, they were stronger in my mouth, the breeze mounting slowly into a full hurricane.

Matthew had begun to laugh at whatever vicious joke he'd made. It seemed he would never stop laughing—at me, at my friend, at everyone.

And then—

The hurricane broke, sending my words pouring toward him, flooding over him with a power that was wholly *other*. I was still whispering, but I directed all the force of that whisper toward no one but him.

He shut his mouth. His laughter cut off.

But I kept going. I didn't care that I had stopped him. It wasn't enough.

I spoke again, my words musical, this time filling my voice with the scars he'd inflicted on the victims before me. I didn't know their names, and I wish I could say that I did this for them. But I didn't. I did it for me. I wanted to wound him.

More. More. *More.* A tsunami of power rushed through me.

I whispered that nobody loved him. I said he was unworthy. I told him—I hated myself for all of it, but I couldn't stop—I told him he deserved to suffer.

Distantly, I was aware that everyone around us had slowed down. Some wore expressions of sadness, some of confusion or pain. They were hearing it too, but only the barest echo of what I directed at Matthew. The world around us slipped into slow motion in the undertow of my words. Even the snowflakes fell more slowly, tentatively.

Matthew started walking toward me, almost hypnotized. I was singing by that point, a quiet melody. He heard me across the distance. And he listened.

Maybe he thought if he could get to me, he could silence me. Maybe he thought he could explain. Or sink into nothingness. I don't know.

He walked into the street.

I broke off my song, just as the screeching sound of a car's brakes woke me from my trance.

I stared, heart racing, as the car's driver jumped out of his seat and rushed to Matthew lying on the ground.

"Are you okay?" the driver yelled in panic.

Matthew moaned and cradled his arm, blinking as if waking from a dream. Even from across the street I could see his terror and puzzlement and the lingering, overwhelming sorrow in his eyes.

I stood frozen as adults and children snapped back into motion and gathered around him, calling for an ambulance, yelling that he was going to be okay. The waves of magic ebbed out of me finally, leaving me empty and shaking.

No one turned to look at me. No one seemed to understand what had happened.

I ran.

I ran down the block, away from the school. I flew down the streets toward my home, where I thought maybe I could forget what I'd done. Forget that I'd been right all along—magic was real. I hadn't imagined it two summers before, when Gran had sung out over the ocean and made my heart ache. I hadn't imagined the water swirling around her, sparkling like starlight. Whatever magic Gran had, I must somehow have it too. Except...

I wasn't beautiful and gentle like Gran had been. I was dark and destructive. I was a monster.

I told no one. Neither did Matthew. His arm was broken, his ribs were bruised, he had a mild concussion, but he was healing. He never explained why he stepped in front of that car. Did he not know? Not remember? I wasn't sure. But he got quieter after that, and he never taunted Sara or me again.

Everyone else seemed to shrug it off too. No one mentioned that strange, slow moment before the screeching of the car. No one mentioned the sudden memory of every unkind thing they'd ever done.

They all might have forgotten, but I remembered. I lived with it, every day and night. I tried to tell myself Matthew deserved it, I was meting out justice. I knew that was a lie.

Because even though I was horrified at what I'd done, and even though I swore to never let that power take over again... I wanted to. There was a voice inside me whispering, *You are special. You can use this.*

I hated that part of me. And yet it called to me. And I couldn't let Mom or Dad or Gran or anyone else know.

In the meantime, my parents kept drifting apart. No one had said the word *divorce* yet, but I knew it was coming. My world was a sandcastle crumbling in the rising tide.

I grasped at a single hope: If I watched Gran more closely the next summer, maybe I could learn how she controlled herself. I waited for summer with a certain sort of desperation. When we drove off to our vacation, Dad didn't hug Mom goodbye. When Mom and I spilled out of the car at the end of the long, hot drive and dived right into Gran's hugs and gentleness, I held on extra tight. And when the tears came, she patted me on the shoulder and said it would be okay. I think she meant things with my parents, but I could only hope she meant with me as well.

I couldn't bring it up. Not then, and not for a week after we arrived. I couldn't bear the idea that someone I loved so much would soon know the monster I'd become.

So I put it off and watched her like I had the summer before—waiting to catch her at something magical, only this time I hoped to learn the secret to her goodness too.

I don't know what finally woke me one night, but something pulled me from the undertow of sleep and pushed me out of bed. I slipped from my room and crept down the hallway. The light of the full moon shone through the living room curtains and drew me outside. At least... I thought it was the light, but then I heard singing. I followed it to the beach, and there was Gran, calling out to sea.

I crouched behind the rock I'd used before, listening. The music drew me, pleaded with me to hear. The wind blew stronger, and the waves grew higher. I listened and watched the ocean swell and somehow stood my ground as my hope swelled too.

Gran wasn't hurting anyone, she was just singing. She was in control of herself, the power flowing through—instead of overwhelming—her.

The music went on and on, hours maybe, I didn't know. I yawned, sleepily drifting on the soothing melody. My limbs felt heavy, and I yearned for home and my bed. Still Gran sang, and I smiled. I would ask her the next day. I didn't need to be afraid. I would break my silence and confess what I'd done, and Gran would forgive me and love me still because she was good and kind. She could teach me control.

Tomorrow, I told myself. *Tomorrow I will do all of that.* But for that night, the music had lulled me into peace. I crawled back to bed and fell asleep, the smile still on my face.

I heard about the boat the next day. Gran was sleeping in after what Grandpa called "a long night"—surely all those hours of singing—and Grandpa was absorbed in his crossword puzzle. I was practically bouncing with the anticipation of finally talking to Gran, and Mom decided she needed to get me out of the house so I didn't wake Gran with my fidgeting. So we wandered into town for brunch, and I endured the waiting. Gran was going to help me, after all, and all would be well.

We stopped at our favorite diner and sat at a table with a newspaper left behind by the previous customer. Our food came, and somewhere between my first tumbler of OJ and my fifth mouthful of waffle, I noticed the headline.

"Seven Die in Mysterious Shipwreck."

I stopped chewing. My eyes flew across the words of the story. Just after midnight the previous night, a sudden storm had blown in, and a vessel had veered off course and crashed. Then, even stranger, instead of radioing for help or grabbing flotation devices, all seven men aboard the ship simply... drowned.

"How awful," Mom said, noticing where my attention had gone. "That's less than a mile from the house."

I could barely swallow anymore, the food clogging my throat. I remembered the waves building in the ocean. Gran's strange, resonating voice that seemed to call to me. I was like those people around Matthew when I sang to him—merely catching a hint of what the song had intended. I imagined the full force of its plea reaching a tiny fishing ship, begging them to find peace. To sleep.

I'd thought her song was gentle, bittersweet. But suddenly I could feel how my own contentment that night had been unnatural. I could see how its full measure might send a sailor to a watery death.

A word had sat on the edge of my mind ever since I'd sung Matthew into the road. I hadn't thought it when Gran sang, but it had been intruding ever since February. But with the news of a mysterious shipwreck sitting in front of me, the word was back, filling my head with a music I didn't want to hear.

We'd had a monthlong unit on mythology the previous year in Ms. Cowan's class, but even without that, I would have known. I'd always had a fascination with the monsters of the world: werewolves, basilisks, ghouls... sirens.

I hadn't known my fascination was because of the monster in me. And suddenly, I knew it was in Gran too.

I'd counted on her to save me, but how could one monster save another? We were both lost.

I shuddered, the orange juice sloshing in my stomach. "I want to go home," I whispered.

Mom looked at my still-full plate and up at my face. "Are you feeling sick?" She reached to feel my forehead.

I shook my head. "Can we go home?"

She signaled the server. "Of course. Gran can whip you up one of her smoothies."

I shuddered again, cringing. "No! Not Gran. I want to go back to our real home."

Mom shrugged and said we'd talk about it—in that way that parents do when they think you'll forget and they won't have to deal with it later. But of course I wouldn't forget.

My mind spun as we walked back to my grandparents' house. There had to be a way out of the conclusions I'd come to. I didn't want Gran to be a siren. But as soon as I thought it, some part of me marrow-deep knew that she was, knew that *I* was. This was who we were, and I had to run away from it. The air was pressing in, and any moment the call, that *music*, would curl its way inside me like tentacles, wrapping around my bones and drowning me.

It took three days. Three days to convince Mom I was not going to snap out of my mood. Three days of cowering in the guest bedroom at the cottage, avoiding contact with anyone during the day, tossing and turning at night. And when I finally slept, I saw sailors, their eyes glazed, empty smiles on their faces as they stepped off the side of their boat or simply drifted off to endless sleep.

I spent those days afraid I'd hear the voice again, afraid of Gran, afraid of myself. If Gran was a siren, did Grandpa know? Was he under her spell? What other horrors had I not yet discovered?

I sifted through every memory I had of Gran during those three days, searching for understanding. All the love and light that had filled my summers warred against the absolute certainty of who and what we were—and the knowledge of that shipwreck. Nothing made any sense, but I could see no other explanation beyond Gran and her terrible, beautiful song.

I thought of all the sandcastles we'd built on the beach. The food that always tasted better when we ate it on the porch, watching the ocean. Her hugs, so soft and enveloping. I'd felt safe in them, safe in ways that I rarely felt out in the real world, where everything was bright and loud and fast. When she hugged me, it was warm and quiet. My muscles relaxed. I could just be.

Our last hug that summer when she wrapped her arms around me right before I dodged into Mom's car to leave—even then, everything felt softer and safer. She had worried over me in those three days, trying everything to soothe and comfort, but I wouldn't be drawn in. It wasn't fair that she still felt like safety and love. It wasn't right.

I cried all the way home.

But I couldn't cry forever, not even at that age. Eventually I had to think. Eventually I had to decide what to do. Once the initial horror had ebbed, the obvious choice was to talk to my mother. Maybe I had misunderstood what I'd seen, what I thought I knew. I was too young to make sense of Gran and magic and death. If I could turn it over to someone else, everything would be all right.

But... Mom was running ragged. I had seen her crying while she sat at the computer and paid bills. I had heard her up late, sniffling over wedding albums.

And what if she didn't believe me? I was already in therapy to deal with the changes in our lives. What if she told my therapist and they thought I was making it up? Worse yet, what if they found out about me too?

I couldn't find the words to explain anything. Every time I tried, I only found another reason not to, and my worries wrapped around me like seaweed, dragging me down. When the questions swirling around me became nearly unbearable, I finally reached a decision—or rather, I chose to defer the decision for as long as I could.

I would stop trying to find a way to tell my story. That wasn't working. But I would watch. If other ships wrecked mysteriously, if there were unexplained injuries or accidents in the news, I would not be silent again.

I would confront her and beg for answers, plead with her to stop. It was terrifying to think of—what if she turned against me? What if she tried to hurt me too? I believed that she loved me and would never hurt me, but I'd also believed she was good and kind and perfectly ordinary. If I was wrong about that, I could be wrong about the love too. I had to be prepared—which was the final part of my plan.

If I talked to her and she couldn't be reasoned with, someone had to stop her. The police couldn't do it, she could control them with her voice. She could control anyone.

Anyone *except* maybe me.

So as much as I had sworn to myself I would never sing again, I could see no other way out. I still felt a pull, whispering along my skin like a breeze—*I had power*. Gran had controlled the ocean with it, had sent people to their deaths. What could I do if I dared?

But I had to learn to control that impulse and harness it somehow. It was another bit of mythology come to life. I was sailing between my own personal Scylla and Charybdis. If I could not force myself to learn this skill, I would not be safe from Gran in a confrontation. But if I gave in to temptation, I would lose myself in the music. Sail too far in either direction, and I would drown.

I started out small, with strangers. It seemed safest that way—I wouldn't be tempted to torture them for any little perceived slight.

So I sat on a bench after school one day, watching the children play, and I saw a girl who looked a little lonely, a little shy.

I'd never tried to sing this way on purpose, but I found somehow that when I opened my mouth, I knew instinctively how to do it. It wasn't singing exactly so much as it was... impossible to describe. Like humming, but with words. Like wishes running through your head but made into sound. I whisper-sang to that girl: *"Have fun, go make a friend."*

She stood. She'd been sitting alone in the corner of the playground, digging in the sand, but I watched as she walked over to a little boy climbing on the ropes. She said something to him, he nodded, and they ran together toward the slides. Exhilaration rose as a tide within me. *I did that.*

Waves of power crashed against my edges, pushing to be set free. I could do more. I had changed this girl for a day, but she would run back to her old familiar stream of shyness after I left. But I—I could wash away the channels and create a wholly new path. I could *make* her something new.

It was tempting, so tempting. The pressure built inside like summer rain clouds, heavy and just a breath away from bursting. I opened my mouth to sing again. It would be good for her, she would be happy.

But I thought of Matthew. I thought of the ships. I thought of the monstrous thing I never wanted to be. I dug my fingernails into my palms to distract me, and I kept my lips closed, my teeth gritted together, waiting as the magic ebbed away and the girl climbed up the ladder and flew down the slide and laughed with her new friend.

I shook with power and fear and adrenaline, a heady mix. I hadn't gone too far. I knew it wasn't right, not even this small thing, making the girl do something against her will. But... it hadn't hurt her. I hadn't hurt anyone. Maybe I could do this after all.

The magic got easier after that. Like it had always been inside me, waiting to burst through a dam I hadn't known about until it broke. I tried it at the mall, in my therapist's waiting room, on a walk through a park—little nudges, nothing too significant, still sailing a delicate line.

I wish I could say it got easy to *stop* the magic too when it welled and pooled around me, begging to be used. But it has never been that simple. Still, I practiced, I learned, and I did not succumb to the torrent of power. That had to be enough.

Mom broke tradition that year. It was our first Christmas without Dad, and I don't think she could bear the idea of sitting in our tiny apartment, just the two of us, missing him. So she decided we would visit the grandparents instead.

They greeted us like they always did, smiling and full of hugs. I stayed up every night that week, not listening for Santa or presents being placed under the tree. Instead, I listened for the creak of floorboards, waiting to hear my grandmother sneak outside to kill.

She never did.

I could have talked to her then. I *should* have talked to her. But such things are always easier said than done, and I was still only fourteen, and all my worries crowded in and silenced my voice.

I told myself I wasn't ready yet. I wasn't strong enough. I told myself I didn't need to yet. I'd been watching the news so carefully, and all had been quiet since summer. So I kept my silence.

The days passed, Mom and I went back home, and life went on. I ate and slept better, and the pull of the music gentled. I knew I could control it, and that knowledge brought peace. My therapist was proud of how I was "adjusting"—to the divorce, supposedly. If only she knew the truth. I started to relax, just a little, when I turned on the news. It had been months, and the stories I feared had never made their appearance.

I began to hope. For whatever unknown reason, Gran had stopped. We'd both made terrible mistakes, but that was the past. Gran was good, I was good, we were good little sirens, living good little lives. It had been our destiny to destroy and drown, but... we could change our destiny. We didn't have to be monsters ever again.

And then, two months after we got home from Gran's, when hope had built too much, I heard another news story about mysteriously drowning sailors. And after that another. And another.

And I couldn't hope any longer. Whatever peace I had made with the music, she hadn't. Why not? It had been hard to learn control, but I had done it. Why hadn't Gran? It was a question that plagued me.

In the end, the answer didn't matter. She had chosen to be a monster, and I couldn't let it continue. When summer came, I would be ready to stop her, no matter the cost.

Gran died on the fifth of May that year.

Grandpa called my mom, and I heard the wavering in his voice as he spoke. When Mom hung up, she leaned against the wall and began to cry. I went to her, wrapped my arms around her. "She's gone," Mom whispered as we held tight and a maelstrom of emotion rose in me.

Mom and I cried as we packed two suitcases and drove to the coast. The same trip we'd taken so many times before, but this time was so different. We cried as we got out of the car and rushed to hug Grandpa. We cried when none of us could get the smoothies or corn to taste quite right. When Grandpa scattered Gran's ashes to the sea and old people I'd never met hugged me and told me they'd miss her and when neighbors brought casseroles. Even with all the crying and worrying I'd done in the past two years, I'd never cried like this. Rivers of tears. Oceans of tears.

But some of my tears were secretly relief. I felt like I was taking my first full breath since that first boat accident. I would not have to confront Gran, to hold her accountable for what she'd done. She could not hurt anyone else.

A ship crashed on the shore on the fourteenth of May.

It was a larger vessel than any of the others, but the same mysterious circumstances. And suddenly I didn't know what to believe anymore. Again.

What was true? I had been so certain it was Gran, had turned my entire existence toward this one belief. Yet... had I spent her last weeks and months fearing her, preparing to fight her, while she had never been a monster at all? I was unmoored in high seas, lost and alone, trying to stay afloat in the ocean of my confusion and sorrow.

I went to the water to seek solace. I sat on the rock by the beach, the same one I'd hidden behind that summer three years earlier, though it felt much longer than that.

Grandpa came to sit beside me and put his arm around my shoulder. We watched in silence as the sun set into the water and the stars came out, and though the sound of the waves calmed me, it offered no answers to all the questions building in my mind.

The questions pressed in and pressed in until I couldn't bear the silence any longer. "Did you know about Gran?" I finally blurted. "That she was a siren?" It was a relief to say the word aloud.

His eyes widened in surprise, but not in disbelief. After a moment, he nodded. "Yes, I knew."

He knew. It was true. "But if you knew, why...?" There were too many ways to finish the question. Why did you stay with her? Why didn't you stop her? Or, since I was no longer even certain whether Gran was involved in the shipwrecks at all, What is the truth? "Why didn't you tell me?" I finally whispered.

He stared at me like I was one of his crosswords, something to puzzle out, and suddenly he discovered the answer. "You have it too," he whispered, almost a question but not quite.

I could only nod.

He wrapped his arm around me and pulled me closer. "I'm so sorry."

"I don't understand." I sobbed into his shoulder. "Did Gran sink all those ships? If so, what about the one last night? I need to understand," I pleaded.

"Oh, sweetie. No, it wasn't her."

I held my breath, a storm swirling inside.

"I guess I should start at the beginning." He stroked my hair, and the storm calmed a little. "Your gran and I did meet by the ocean, the way we always told you. She was... breathtaking. Would've followed her anywhere."

I thought of sailors walking into the waves. "Was she controlling you? Singing?"

He laughed—actually laughed at the idea. "No. It's just who she was. I didn't believe in love at first sight, still don't really, but there was *something*. Then I made her laugh. That was it for both of us. Never looked back. She said she'd never understood what it meant to be human until she met me."

I hated to ask, but... "How do you know she *wasn't* controlling you?"

He laughed even harder, but I could see tears too. "She tried a few times when she was mad. Oh"—he shook his head—"she hated it when I wouldn't obey. Couldn't understand it. But I'd had this accident as a kid that damaged my hearing. We figured I couldn't hear the magic's frequency or something. Caught an echo of it here and there, though. Boy, was it potent."

I grimaced. Too potent. "But you married her anyway?" It didn't make sense.

"That was just in the beginning. After she realized what it was like for regular people to be under her spell, she stopped using it. Bit of an adjustment," he said wryly, "doing the human thing. She'd spent centuries out there with her sisters—the other sirens, I mean—sleeping for decades, waking up and crashing ships for a while, sleeping again, never caring about anything."

"So she did wreck ships." The knowledge that I'd been right after all was no comfort.

He nodded his head. "Back then, yes. But not for more than fifty years, not since she broke away." He told me how Gran had first left her sisters to experience something new, sort of take her own personal vacation, and that's when she met Grandpa, married him, and began to change.

"Little things at first," he said. "She had aches she'd never had before, human stuff. She started aging. We'd never heard of that before, but then again we'd never heard of any of it. We were making it up as we went along." He went silent, reminiscing.

But I was impatient and had to immediately understand it all. "And?"

"I worried she'd miss immortality. She'd just pull me out on the porch to dance, and she said she'd rather have one more dance with me than a thousand on her own. All that sappy old-person stuff."

I'd seen them dancing that way all through my childhood, but at this, I imagined them young and beautiful with years ahead of them, and it pulled an unwilling smile from me.

He stared into the stars with an answering smile. "Didn't think we could have kids. We were stupid—but still so happy when your mom came along. Little bit scared too. What if your gran's abilities came through?" He shrugged. "Never did, though. We watched her and never saw any signs. Worried less about you, and I guess we didn't pay enough attention. Sorry we didn't see it. Sorry she isn't here to explain everything to you."

I was sorry too and sorry I hadn't asked. These past months could have been so, so different. I shook my head to dispel the thought. "*You're* here, though."

He nodded and squeezed me closer. "I am."

"So tell me the rest."

"Never moved away from the shore. Her sisters fell back asleep after she left them. Not exactly the closest sibling relationship."

I snorted.

"We lived those years as happy and full as we could. Once in a while she'd go out to the water and sing, just to feel it again—not to hurt anyone, just to make the ocean dance."

I remembered that summer, that first night I'd heard her, the way the water swirled around her so wild and free. She hadn't been calling to me, but I wondered... Did it awaken something in me all the same? The fever—Was that my magic coming to life?

"Then a year or so back, she started to feel them in her head. They were stirring. Your gran couldn't let them do their thing anymore. She eventually went out to sing to them, see if she could send them back to sleep."

"The night before the first shipwreck," I said, thinking back to how Gran's song had begged me to go home, to rest. I'd thought her call had been to the sailors.

He nodded, then sighed. "Didn't go too well."

Seven dead.

But it hadn't been Gran after all—she'd tried to stop it. Relief crashed over me.

"Don't really know how it works, all the siren stuff. Just know she fought them, and it tired her out—so many nights out there singing." He swallowed hard and rubbed his hand down his face. "I think that's what killed her," he whispered. "All that fighting. And I couldn't do a thing to help her."

I felt his helplessness at being caught up in this magical world, unable to protect the one he loved. I squeezed his hand and leaned my head on him. "You were there for her."

He nodded against my hair, saying nothing else.

We sat silently, and the waves washed on the beach, and the breeze blew the spray gently on my face, and I tasted salt and felt the heavy pressure of the storm inside me dissipating.

I felt light. I smiled, even with the tears streaming down my face. It was crazy, it was stupid. I had just found out she'd spent the last of her life battling supernatural creatures, but... she was my grandmother again. She was exactly who I had always thought she was, only more. How could I not be grateful?

There would be time for more sadness, plenty of it, and time for regret and guilt at all I had done wrong and every moment I had missed and time for anger at the sisters who took her away from me. But in this moment, joy lapped gently around me, sparkling like water in the moonlight.

And then with a start, I realized something. I pulled away from him. "They're still out there."

He nodded.

"So what happens next?"

"They wreak havoc for a while. They get bored and go back to sleep." He clenched his fists. "Nothing to do but wait it out."

I closed my eyes against that thought. How could we wait it out? There had to be something... And then I realized what should have been obvious from the start. "No." I shook my head slowly, the thought welling in my mind. "There's nothing *you* can do about it."

His gaze sharpened on me. "This isn't your job."

Eddies of power lapped around my soul. "Then whose?" I asked softly.

"They'll stop soon enough."

"No, they won't stop soon enough." I thought of all those helpless sailors drowned in the waves. "It's *already* not soon enough."

"You can't," he said, suddenly worried. "You're too young. They're too powerful." He took my hand in his soft, leathery one, his eyes filling with tears. "I can't lose you too."

I looked away. Maybe he was right. I was too young. They would sleep eventually, no matter what I did. This wasn't my battle.

I stared out at the water as the night grew darker, and I remembered all the gifts my grandmother had given me. Our magical summers. Her endless love, deeper and wider than the ocean. Her goodness, finally and officially reclaimed. She was not a monster, and I did not have to be.

I crawled into bed that night worn down but cleansed too, a bit of sea glass polished by the battering of the waves.

I woke up hours later, suddenly alert, my heart pounding as I tried to discover what woke me. And then I heard it. A song, gorgeous and deadly, drifting on the breeze. A song I couldn't ignore.

All those months I'd spent practicing my music, I'd thought it would be for Gran. And in a way it was. But in the end it wouldn't be to fight against her—I would fight *with* her, continue the battle she hadn't won. Maybe I wouldn't win either, but at least I had to try. And if I stopped even one death, it would be worth it.

I slipped out of bed, out of the house, and walked to the edge of the water. It rolled in cold ripples across my toes, and I closed my eyes to feel the sand, the sea, the air around me. It all became crystal sharp as the power rose like a tide, and I opened my mouth and began to sing.

The music swept through me, building like the wind before a hurricane. The water swelled in response to my voice, shifting and swirling as it flowed around me. I lifted my hands to the sky the way I'd seen Gran do, and I could swear I felt her there beside me, her hand in mine to lend me strength. And I think she was smiling.

The Promise of Snow

IVANA HATED IT HERE. It had been only six days by the calendar of this world, but already she hated it. Her skin itched; sweat trickled between her shoulder blades. When she reached behind her to swipe it away, these inflexible human arms could not reach the spot. When she scratched, she scraped away the last tufts of her fur, leaving them in a growing heap as if she'd shed not just her skin but her self. And when the fur pulled away, it revealed pale new skin—human skin—soft but still itching.

Her pathetic claws now couldn't even draw blood—another cruelty of her transformation in this world. She would prefer scrapes and blood to this incessant itch.

And the heat. The heat was unbearable. She breathed it in. It sank in through her eyes, slithered around her shoulders and neck like a living thing. There was no avoiding it. She had not known that she could feel this way, did not want to know it now. During the day, she wandered this new place. The vivid colors she had so admired as she stared at them from her own world now felt too bright. She had to squint just to look at the flowers growing in profusion underfoot, pinks and reds and yellows clashing all around her. Above, vines of purple and green climbed up trees so immense she could barely see their tops.

Night brought tantalizing fantasies of the beloved world she'd left behind. She dreamed of frozen places, of the expanses of brilliant white, the ice nearly blinding in the radiance of the cold winter sun. She felt the breeze blow through her fur, across her nose. She howled at the moon. But here in this otherworld—when she woke up, here she was drenched in sweat, the heat a physical weight upon her, pushing her down into the vibrant green moss she slept on.

She was tired and sore and broken down. She should have listened when they told her she did not know what it would be like in the otherworld. They said she'd be alone, that there would be no one to care for her. But still she'd watched through the ice, seen the otherworld reflected in the magic of the frozen water. How could she not be curious? The colors in that image blazed. Home was blue and black and gray and white. Here the colors popped around her, and what had seemed so fascinating and magical from across the ice now seemed only overwhelming, too garish, pounding into her head through her eyes until she closed them and breathed a sigh of relief as she saw home once again in her mind. Soon enough, though, she would have to open her eyes to reality again, a reality that she knew she had chosen.

She believed that knowledge would drive her mad.

Only a day into her sojourn in this land, she'd thrown herself into the lake, flailing through the water, seeking for a glimpse of the gate that might take her back home. She could not see it, so she knew it wasn't open, but she continued to splash anyway, desperate for the gate to appear and swallow her back.

It didn't.

Finally she'd dragged herself back out of the water and dropped to the ground, panting. She would never have gone into the water like that in her world, in her previous body. It would have been death, and she would not seek that end to her torment. After all, there was still hope that there might be a way back. There had to be a way back, and she would look until she found it. She kept that hope like a single snowflake fallen to the ground, careful not to breathe too deeply as she gazed at it—lest it melt away.

She didn't hear him approaching as she knelt beneath a tree, picking berries that she had seen the creatures, the humans, gather and eat. She was used to keener hearing that would alert her to danger; it was another thing that she could not have foreseen about this strange world—she felt almost deaf, though she was surrounded by sounds. Birds called in the trees, monkeys howled to one another, the underbrush crackled with her every movement. Yet there was a muteness to her hearing now, a loss of the crystal clarity that allowed her to locate a startled rabbit or keep off the creaking ice.

He was standing almost directly over her before she felt his presence. She turned and cried out, a wordless bark, and startled away from him. But her legs betrayed her, and she fell backward, helpless and vulnerable. He came after her quickly, and though it was not her custom to submit without a fight, she cringed before him.

He did not growl, though, or claw or bite. Of course, she remembered, that is not the way of things here. But still, she had seen enough in her prowling around the village that though men did not growl and claw, there were other ways to hurt. She had quickly learned the words for and uses of knives and fists. It was part of why she resisted going there; she did not want to be known to these creatures she did not yet understand. Still, it was not with violence that he approached her. He bent to his knee, his hand reaching out, and she flinched away from him.

"Are you well?" he asked. Ivana had been surprised, at first, to discover how the language of humans came so simply to her. It must have been the magic of the ice gate.

She merely shuddered, and the places where her fur used to be prickled.

He looked at her more closely and seemed to recognize something in her expression, for he did not immediately try to touch her again. "I'm sorry," he soothed, "I didn't mean to startle you."

She'd seen him before. When she was young and had first started watching the humans through the ice, they'd all looked the same, all furless skin and many-colored coverings. Beautiful, breathtaking, but all vaguely the same beautiful. As she came back to the ice each year to watch them, though, she began to recognize the differences. They grew and changed and had personalities, just as her pack did. One with a mane that grew longer and blacker every year. Another who had skipped and laughed one year—but the next year, she came only to drink, and she never smiled. Two who always came together, holding hands and growing old.

She came to know them in a way, those who came to the water, though she did not know their names or all the reasons that they came. To them, the water seemed a place of play. As she'd watched them, she had thought, perhaps naively, that they must be very immune to cold to splash and laugh in the waters. To her pack, water was always potential death. You did not play in it.

Especially not in this lake, the gate lake.

Of course now she knew that their lake was not the frozen expanse that hers was. Water came in all temperatures, and this water—like all things in this sweltering place—was warm. True, it was cooler than the air, but it could not refresh her; it simply added to the constant heated damp. Even the rain here, of which there was far too much, was not cold. It came down from heavy clouds in sheets, forming tiny rivers through the mud beneath her feet. These humans would splash right through it, going on with their days, taking time to play even as the rain poured down on them. And as they'd played, she'd watched, for many years until the day she had finally built her courage and jumped.

This man standing before her hadn't stood out at first when she'd watched them, but she'd grown used to the people she saw, so she recognized him. He often came to the lake on the single day each year that she could look through into this world. He would fill a jar with water and leave quietly. He laughed occasionally, when the play was funny, but mostly he just went about his business. What he did on his other days, she could not know. Up close and in person now, she saw how his tree-colored hair curled softly against his head, slightly damp from the day's rain shower. His eyes, also dark like the trees that stretched above them, were filled with concern. His voice was soothing like a cool breeze across her skin.

Though she still feared him, still feared so many things in this sweltering place, she felt her breathing begin to slow. The sweat that slicked her palms lessened. Her heart stopped racing, and she felt a moment's calm. In spite of herself, she responded to his concern.

"There is nothing that you can do," she said, shaking her head.

Again he reached out his hand, and this time she took it and allowed him to help her to her feet. "I'm sorry. I wish there was." He spoke with a voice she suspected he would use on a wild animal. Not far from the truth, she thought. "Can I at least offer you something to eat?" He stepped away and pulled off a pack he carried behind him. Still watching her carefully, he brought a leaf-wrapped pastry from his pack and showed it to her. "It's not much."

The smell of meat wafted from the leaves, and her mouth watered. Yes, it was cooked meat, but her new human body seemed to wish for that. She had eaten only meagerly since her arrival.

"Thank you."

He nodded and watched as she devoured the meat-filled pastry. He hesitated before asking, "Are you sure there's nothing I can do for you? You are obviously not from here." He gestured to her skin and hair, so many shades paler than everyone she had seen living in the village. "Are you with the traders who just came through? I can help you find them." When she did not respond, he shrugged helplessly. "You seem lost."

Almost she told him the truth then, a sudden instinct to trust overcoming her. But caution stopped her; she could not speak of her home to a stranger. She shook her head again. "I am lost, but you cannot help me." At this, her throat constricted and she turned away.

When he reached out as if to comfort her, she backed away. She could not accept comfort in this terrible place.

He smiled gently, compassion in his eyes. "I'll leave you, then. But if you need my help, I live in the village, at the end of the main street, across from the well. If you can't find me, ask for Tomas the weaver."

She nodded but did not turn around.

"May I ask your name?"

"Ivana," she whispered.

"Goodbye, Ivana. Good luck." The leaves rustled softly, and by the time she turned her head to watch, he was gone.

She felt more bereft then than she had before, and she sat down again, this time to cry salty tears that mingled with the salt of her skin.

She had avoided contact with the humans, preferring to prowl rather than interact. As far as she knew, the man Tomas was the only human who had even seen her. She did not relish the idea of entering the village and finally becoming known to the humans, but even less did she want to die alone, here in this miserable world. So she staggered the short path from the lake to the tiny village, swaying as the colors and sounds seemed to grow brighter, then fade, then swell again.

She'd never followed the dirt path to where it led between the houses of the village, where the rays of sunshine filtered down through the leaves of the jungle and left the forest clearing dappled in sunshine. She felt exposed and vulnerable. Eyes seemed to follow her every step.

A wave of dizziness swept over her, pushing her forward. She knew which house was his from watching the people—there was no need to ask for direction. She also knew the proper greeting, and once she was near his doorway, she clapped. "Tomas?" she called, her voice sounding tinny in her ears.

Immediately he appeared on the doorstep. In one quick look, he assessed her state. He swept forward and picked her up, not bothering to ask permission. The action was none too soon; she'd begun to sway. The light of the sun dimmed as he brought her inside, but it seemed to dim more than it should have, and it was becoming foggy and patched with black. *Strange*, she thought, before she could think no more.

"You've been sick."

Those were the first words Ivana heard when she opened her eyelids, so heavy they felt like stones.

"It's common to traders who come through the jungle for the first time. I'm sorry I didn't think of it when I saw you. I would have insisted you come to the village to be cared for."

She opened her eyes to look for him, and he brushed her forehead with a rag that had been soaked in water. It wasn't precisely cool, but it was more pleasant than much of what she had felt here, and a tentative smile formed on her lips.

He answered her smile with a much wider one of his own. "I'm glad you came before it was too late. Dying of jungle fever, alone and hallucinating, cannot possibly be pleasant." He sat back and appeared to think before adding, "Well, I suppose that depends on the hallucinations."

She chuckled and was immediately surprised by it. It felt so human, not like the laughter of her people.

He chuckled too, reaching out to smooth her hair back as he wiped her forehead again.

She thought to rise, but he stopped her. "No, you should still rest."

And so she did.

Once begun, it was simple to fall in love with Tomas. The instinct to trust him that she'd felt on their first meeting was easy to embrace.

His voice was a trickle of ice through her veins, his laugh a cool breeze. Even the brush of his hand against hers—it was warm, but not with the oppressive warmth of everything here. It was more like curling up with the pack on an especially freezing night. Despite her previous fears, she found herself telling him the truth of her life, wondering how he would receive such news.

"I knew you were not from here," he simply remarked. "The hair, your skin, those pale gray eyes." He touched her cheek, held it. "Of course, I thought maybe from beyond the lake—not from within it." He grinned, and she grinned in return. His smile was that way, an infection that was easily caught.

She took him to the lake one day and showed him. "This is the place I fell into your world, on the day of longest sun. It is the only time one can cross that bridge to your world. It is the only day one can even see it, and even then, some cannot see it at all."

She stared down into the water, imagining her own people there. It was still close to longest sun in both places now, and the ice was at its thinnest, so they would keep away at this time of year. All except for Ivana. She had always slunk away to watch the humans for those hours the tunnel was visible. Each year she wondered if she would have the courage to jump once the vision opened into a gate. She wondered until the day she did it.

Still, though she could not see them, she could imagine them—her pack, prowling for food, tussling together, or nestled in a pile to rest. And beyond them, as far as the eye could see, the expanses of ice and snow. Above them, the sky—cold, gray, beautiful in all its shades of light and dark. Within its clouds, the promise of snow. If she were there, the cold would make her shiver with pleasure, but she was here now, and despite her imagination she could feel only the heat.

"Did you mean to do it?" he asked, breaking her from her reverie.

She sighed reluctantly. "Yes. The legends of my people warn us away from the ice on the day of longest sun. They say those who fall through never return. Most will not stray near the lake, not on any day, except sometimes to hunt fish. But I—" She looked down, remembering. "I would not listen. I watched your world, caught up in its beauty, its color, the leaves and flowers growing everywhere. I saw you there. I would watch you—I mean, I would watch your people." She blushed. "I was determined to discover what it was like." She shrugged. "So I came."

He sat beside her now, his fingers touching her knee as he looked into her eyes. "And is it so bad here?"

She looked away. "It is not all bad."

He waited, but she did not continue. "Except?" he prompted.

She looked up into the sky, the brightness of the noon sun burning the air white. "Except that." She pointed upward. "I could not have known, but I should have known. I was warned. From my world, I could see only the colors—and a sky so bright I could barely look at it. But I could not feel it. I could not feel the scorching heat that burns into your core, setting your blood on fire. Every day I wait to see if my skin will melt from the heat, and every day it does not." She held out her hand before her, staring at it in wonder. "I am almost surprised."

He reached gently to grasp that hand and hold it between his. "And I am deeply glad," he said solemnly.

The heat of his hand, still so different from the heat of the air that constantly pressed in on her, rushed up through her skin. She looked again into his eyes, a deep dark brown like the bark of growing things. He leaned in, and she closed her eyes. When his lips pressed against hers, a glorious fire burned through her. She didn't mind.

His presence complicated things. She'd thought long and hard about how to get back home and had finally come to a conclusion that felt right. This world's longest night was approaching quickly, and if Ivana was correct about the ice gate, this was the time that she would be able to go back home. She knew the stories that no one had ever come back, but she was sure this was the way. If longest day brought her to this land, longest night would take her back home, if she willed it.

"Do your people ever speak stories of a gate to my world?" she asked him one day.

He shook his head, apologetic. "We have plenty of legends and stories, but nothing about your world or a gate in the lake."

She shrugged and looked away as if it didn't matter. She still believed she was right. "Not any tales of your longest night?"

"Nothing," he said, but then he stopped, and his brows drew together. "Wait. I think I remember Matias the storyteller telling of a couple who disappeared that night, many years ago." He waggled his eyebrows. "He says they got lost on the way to... spend some time together. Alone. On the longest night of the year." He winked.

She blushed, a reaction that felt very strange on her skin. At the same time, her heart picked up. She was right, the gate did open that night. She could go home.

But every day she felt his smile. Every day he made her laugh. She could not imagine living here, in this overheated world of endless sunshine where even the rainstorms were streaked with rays of light and left her drenched but no less sweltering.

But she could not imagine living in her beautiful, snowy home without him.

And yet, despite the wrenching in her heart, the day grew closer. Each sunrise brought one less day to make her choice.

He saw the wrenching within her. They sat together in the relative cool of the late evening, their feet dangling into the stream, the heat bearable for the moment. "You're planning to go back, aren't you." It wasn't a question.

She leaned against his shoulder. "I do not know."

He was silent for a moment. Then: "I could come with you," he said quietly.

She lifted her head and stared at him. "You would do this?"

There was fear in his eyes, but he nodded firmly and spoke without hesitation. "I would."

She had not even considered that he might be willing. This opened a new world of possibilities. She jumped up from the ground in excitement. Then, just as quickly, she stopped and dropped back, staring down. "But what of your family? Your business? Your life here?"

He took her shoulders and forced her to look into his eyes. "I will leave them behind for you. You will be my family... If you want me."

She took a shuddering breath. "Of course I want you." Then she shook her head. "But I cannot ask this thing of you. I changed in crossing between our worlds. I became like you. But what if you do not become like me? Or what if my feelings here about the heat—what if those are your feelings about the cold? You will grow to hate it and resent me." She felt hopelessness battle the hope within her. She did not want to examine the possibilities; she just wanted to go.

"I will go with you. We'll work it out together." He smiled, one side of his mouth quirked up in humor. "If I don't change, you will simply have to make me a coat of rabbit skins. If I am always cold, well…" He grinned wider still. "I'm sure you can come up with some way to keep me warm." Then he winked.

Ivana laughed and felt the tension leave her. She did not have to choose between the things she loved most after all.

And so they prepared to leave. There was little to do. Tomas would leave his looms behind, and one of his nephews would take over when it became clear he was not coming back. They would not be telling anyone their plan. Together they visited his friends and relatives, and quietly he bade farewell to the world he had known his whole life. She was as busy as she could be, desperate not to think too deeply about what they were attempting.

But she loved him, and so she watched him, waiting to see the taint of regret. Her dreams became filled with both hope and despair, warring inside her—the hope a soft snow constantly melting under the oppressive sun of despair. But he never wavered, and slowly the snow mounted in her soul until it could not easily be burned off. She began to smile, to sing. Her whole world felt white.

Finally, longest night came. While the people of the village held their wild celebrations of laughter and song and vigils to welcome the night, she and Tomas slipped away into the approaching darkness. They walked up the river until it reached the lake, calm and lapping gently under the light of a full moon.

He took her hand. "This is it."

She nodded. "Are you certain you wish to go?"

He squeezed her hand, and his warmth simmered through her. "You really have to stop asking that, you know. If you ask me again, I might have to kiss you just so you can't speak."

She laughed. "Are you certain you wish to go?"

He grabbed her and kissed her, but she playfully shoved him away. "Fine. I will stop asking." She looked up into the sky. The time didn't feel quite right yet, not the way it had when she crossed this way. That time she had just known when to look down into the lake, known when she would see the gate open up. "I do not think it is time yet," she offered as she began to sit on a rock beside the lake.

He had stepped closer to the water and suddenly sucked in his breath. "No, it's time. I can see it." He took a deeper breath. "Your world is so stark, so beautiful." When he turned to look back at her, his eyes shone. "Like you." He stepped closer, bringing his toe nearer the water. "Come." He beckoned. "Let's not wait anymore."

She stood again. Something was wrong. She stepped toward him. "Wait!" she cried. He stopped, his feet just beside the water.

He turned back and quirked his brow. "What's wrong?"

"Where is it? I cannot see it." She stared frantically down into the water.

He pointed. "Right there, right there beside those rocks."

She stared, squinted. "No. I cannot see it."

He stepped back from the water, looking uncertain for the first time. He pointed again, but she shook her head. Her heart pumped wildly.

"What if... What if your people were right? You can only go one way."

She took his hand and pulled him still farther back. "I cannot see the gate. I can never go back." Her pale skin paled even further as she continued to shake her head. "I could have lost you," she whispered. "You could have stepped into my world and been gone forever."

He turned to face her, reaching out to put his hand on her cheek.

She pulled her hand from his grasp, stepping away from him. Her eyes were wide as the realization crashed through her, burning in seconds through all the drifts of joy that had built in her soul. "I am so very sorry. I was foolish, more even than I was in coming here." She drew back. "I am so sorry," she whispered. Then she turned and crashed headlong through the jungle, heedless of its dangers, only knowing she had to get away from the taunting lake. Its waters lapping against the shore sounded far too much like laughter that she would never see its gate again. She would never be comfortable again. And she had almost sacrificed Tomas to discover it.

She knew you should not wander into the jungle, late at night, by yourself, but her anger and guilt drove her. If she could have run away from herself, she would not have felt the need to run through the dark. But she could not avoid herself, or the thoughts that continued to heap themselves like a physical weight upon her shoulders.

All the things she had avoided thinking about. When Tomas had told her about the man and woman from his land who had disappeared, and when he'd gotten Matias to tell them more stories of disappearances at longest night—a thought had flickered through her. Why had her pack never met any of those who went through the gate? What had happened to them? She hadn't wanted to think of it then, too full of the excitement that Tomas would come with her. But now she thought, and the thoughts felt correct in her mind, the way she'd always instinctively understood the nature of the gate.

The gate would take someone from this world back to the lake on longest night, the coldest and most dangerous night of the year. She knew from experience how to treat such a night, how to protect herself. Even with a transformation, with fur and claws instead of skin and nails, could anyone from Tomas's world of burning sunlight possibly know what to do in burning cold? Worse yet, when she came through the gate, she came through into water. What if they had done the same, coming back perhaps even under the ice? They both would have died, trapped as the water leeched the life from them.

She had nearly killed them both, all because she hated this heat, was not willing to consider the idea of living with it for the rest of her days.

But she considered it now. There was no other choice.

She came back to him late the next morning and stood just inside his doorway. "I am sorry," she said, her eyes on the ground. "I could not accept it, but I must. I risked you, Tomas, for my own selfishness. I did not care that you might be hurt. Had you gone through the gate without me..." She shuddered. "You would have died." She tried to cover her heart in ice for her next words, to tell him she would leave forever if he wanted.

She looked up and for the first time noticed the changes in his house. When they'd left the night before, his belongings were set out and ready for his nephew. Now they were bundled tightly into packages meant for travel. Even his second largest loom was dismantled, packed up. Her eyes ran across it all then raced to him. It seemed she would not need to offer to leave; he was leaving her first.

"You're... going somewhere?" she asked, trying to keep the trembling from her voice.

He shook his head. "No, not me."

She wrinkled her forehead. "I cannot use your loom."

"No, Ivana. Not you either. Us. Together." When she didn't respond, he waved her over and turned to a piece of paper he'd set out on his table. "Look here." He pointed, and when she stepped closer, she could see that it was a drawing of the lake and its surroundings.

She looked where he pointed, at a spot far above the lake.

"Look. I've been asking the elders again, and Matias says that there is a legend of this place. The story is of a land, here on this mountain." She looked again as he pointed to a range of pointed triangles. "You go up the mountains far enough, it is cold. Cold and white, and flakes of coldness fall from the sky there. No one knows where the legend came from, or even if it's true. Matias says long ago groups left the village to learn more, but no one has ever returned." He nodded in excitement. "That is where we are going."

She stared at him.

"It won't be like your home," he added apologetically. "It might not even be real. But it looks promising, yes?"

When she wrapped her arms around him, the flakes of snow began to fall again in her soul.

She woke in the night, her body twisted in the sweat-drenched sheets, her blood burning with remembered heat. Years had come and gone, some slow like the breaking of the ice in early spring, some fast like a sudden blizzard—but the fever still came this way. She rose quietly from the bed, tiptoed away, and stepped outside into the cool air. She could always tell when snow was coming, and on those nights when the fever burned brightest, the cold of the winter burned iciest too.

Standing on her porch, a breeze blowing about her, she lifted her arms, spinning a slow circle as the wind rose. Her hair, pale in the moonlight, shifted in the breeze. She tilted her head up to see the cool face of the moon staring back down at her. Her mouth opened to catch the first snowflake of whatever storm was on its way.

She smiled. The heat had passed again.

She turned to step back inside, but her husband was there, barefoot despite the chill, smiling and watching her.

"Come here," she whispered, and he came to stand beside her in the dark of the night. His arm wrapped around her waist as he pulled her closer. She sighed and closed her eyes. This here, this was the best of everything—the warmth of the pack, the joy of the winter sun, the promise of snow.

The Candlemaker

HERE'S THE THING: It didn't happen quite the way they tell you. I mean, yes, I was his godfather, and yes, he went around selling miracle cures and predicting medical outcomes with surprising accuracy. And maybe I hovered over the deathbeds, watching him work. But I never could tell my boy anything he didn't want to hear, and he definitely didn't marry the princess. What a ridiculous ending that would have been for Death's godson.

It was a dark night when I met his father. I was returning home from my business, tired and worn, when he walked up to me.

He was carrying a baby, which was intriguing. People rarely approach me with children. People don't usually look at me at all.

"You're Death, aren't you?" he asked.

And people hardly ever speak my name above a whisper.

"Yes," I said.

He held his child out so I could see the baby's face. The child squawked and squirmed in his arms.

"Will you be his godfather?" the man asked.

"Will I what?" I must have heard him wrong.

"Be his godfather." There was an edge of desperation to his tone, and he may have been a little drunk. "Here's what I think: God, he rewards people for being good. Satan, he punishes people for being bad. You—you just do the same thing to everyone no matter what. You're *fair*." He emphasized this last word like the world should bow down and submit all to the idea of *fairness*. Like everything would just make sense as long as it was *fair*. Maybe he was a little more drunk than I'd realized.

But I wasn't about to argue if he liked me best. That's pretty rare for me. Besides, I like expanding my horizons, trying new things. Maybe godfathering would suit me. "I suppose I can do that," I said slowly. "What exactly does a godfather do?"

He got a little vague after that. "I don't know," he said. "I guess you sort of teach him to be a good person and kind of fill in where I'm lacking..." He shrugged and looked away. I think he was beginning to realize he hadn't thought this through very well. Or maybe the drink was wearing off.

"Oh, that's fine. I can do that. No problem at all."

I was perhaps a bit too optimistic.

That little baby was cute, sure, but as soon as he could toddle and talk, he started showing up at my shop. (I couldn't help but think his parents seemed to have a pretty lax attitude toward parenting, letting their toddler hang around with Death all the time.) I'd have a full rack of candles dipping into my giant vat of simmering wax, and he'd wander in and start *touching everything*. Any normal kid would stay away from me and my candles. But not my little godson; he never seemed to be bothered by any of it.

I tried not to, but I think I loved him a little bit for that.

"Godfather Death, what are you doing?" he would ask, his eyes wide and his fingers reaching out to grab at the sharp scissors at my worktable. I swatted his hand away.

"Making candles." Obviously.

He picked up a spool of wicking and started unraveling it onto the floor. "Why?"

"It's my job." I snatched it from his hands and wound the cord up again. I placed it back on a higher shelf this time.

"Why?" He'd knocked over a pile of wax blocks by this point, and I was restacking them.

"Because it is."

"Why?"

"It just is." I snatched the scissors from his hands (again) and picked him up. I plopped him on a stool, blessedly far from any of my equipment. "Here, you sit here and watch."

I showed him the candle wax bubbling over the fire and the wicks hanging from the poles, waiting to be dipped and cooled.

"What are they for?"

Finally. A question I could answer.

And I began to explain to him. Each candle, I told him, is a human life. The wick determines the length of that life—long wicks, long burn, long life. The more that I dipped the candle, the fatter it would become—and the richer the individual's life, more abundant in joy and blessings and whatever sort of successes life had in store. Living wasn't particularly my business, so I didn't bother much with the details.

The trickiest bit was the wick's treatment. I prepared each wick carefully so that it would burn with different colors of flame. The colors told the story of how each human life would end. Length, quality, and ending, all contained in the burning of the candle. An elegant system, if I do say so myself.

I thought that would satisfy him, but the questions never ended.

As he got older, they at least became more interesting. "What did that flame mean? How long is that wick? How do you know how to make the candle?" I tried to bog him down in technical details, but nothing ever stopped his insatiable curiosity.

He came around so much that I finally got used to the questions and started volunteering extra information. One day I took him into the burning room—the room off of my workshop where were lit all the candles of the living. He looked around in wonder. A vast hall stretched before us, endless rows of candles, endless in their variety and beauty, each colored flame glowing, flickering, lighting up its little sphere. Such a large room should not have fit into my back closet, but that is the least of Death's magic.

He approached a shelf of candles and carefully lifted one. "So with this candle, I can know all about this person? I can tell when she will die and how?"

I nodded.

He looked around again, and his eyes fixed on a small shelf set apart from the others. On it was a candle whose violet flame didn't melt its wax. I should have known he'd see that one immediately. Too smart for his own good, that kid. I made a mental note to hide a few of the candles that he really shouldn't see. "Whose candle is that?" he asked.

"Maybe I'll tell you someday. But for now, out!" And I shooed him from the room and sent him on his way.

The years passed, and as they went, his family fell into poverty. His parents had work, but they always managed to drink away their profits (drunkenness was not, apparently, a state saved only for special occasions like a baby's birth). His siblings, who did not have the fortune of my superior tutelage—who I'd never even met, despite my offering of friendship—followed suit. Only my boy saved his pennies and stayed sober.

Over time, the boy's questions became more detailed and pointed, but I was happy to answer. After all, I didn't have a whole lot of interesting company coming around.

Then one day he asked if I would help him with something. This was not his usual sort of question, so I was curious. But suspicious too. People don't usually ask Death for help.

"What do you need?" I asked.

He looked down at his feet, awkward. I'd never seen him shy before. "I have a dream," he finally said. "I dream of never being cold again, never having to beg for food or clothing again. I want to be able to afford anything I desire." He lifted his chin in defiance. "And I dream more than that. I'm going to be famous. People will know my name and speak of me with awe."

Quite an impressive dream, I thought, and despite myself, I was intrigued. I waited.

"And with your help, I can make it happen," he added.

"Oh really?" I asked. "And how is that?"

He then explained his plan. Apparently he was going to become a famous doctor—or maybe a wizard. He wasn't exactly clear on the distinction. The point is, people would call on him when they were sick, and they'd pay him ridiculous amounts of money for a cure. And his predictions about their health would be uncannily accurate.

That, of course, was where I came in, with my candles. When he got called to a household where someone was sick, he would first stop by my shop and check the candles in the burning room. He'd find out if the person was destined to die or recover. If the patient was destined to live, he'd administer his curative tonic.

He had to have a tonic, you know, and the more disgusting the better. The nastier the medicine, the more that people believed in it.

Of course, if the patient was destined to die, he planned to shake his head sadly and say, "Some things even magic cannot cure." Then, just out of the kindness of his heart, he'd give them some other sort of glop for free, something to ease the pain of passing. Because the goodwill of the bereaved would be good for business.

He'd get rich off of his magical "cures," he'd be famous for his knowledge of the future, and he'd never want for anything again.

At first, of course, he couldn't just show up as a magical healer. No one would be crazy enough to admit some strange young man without any credentials. So his plan was that when he heard about someone sick in the area, he would invent some sort of errand to the house, and then he'd make an offhand comment to someone nearby. "Oh, it's obvious he has the consumption. Poor fellow, going to die within the week." Or, "I can't believe everyone is so uptight about this case. She's going to be just fine." That sort of thing. Given enough opportunities, enough unexpected outcomes that he predicted correctly, the boy was sure that people would start looking to him for advice—and then he'd start charging.

"It's going to take a long while," I said once he'd finished his explanation. "A reputation like that isn't made overnight."

He nodded, unfazed. "I know. But I can do it." Then he really stared into my eyes—a feat which, I should mention, very few people could comfortably manage. "I can do it... if you will help me."

I sat back and thought for a few moments. He had thought this plan through, and I suspected it would suit me nicely as well. I waited long enough that the boy started to look a little uncomfortable. No sense in making it easy for him. "Sure," I finally said, "I'll play along."

And it worked. There were a few bumps, of course. At first, no one was paying any attention to his predictions. The unknown messenger who drops by with a note from a neighbor and comments on someone's health—he doesn't get much notice.

In fact, my boy was getting a little desperate until he heard about the local baron's illness. Everyone expected this man to die. Honestly, if I hadn't dipped his candle in the first place, I would have too. He lived a life of terrible eating, worse drinking, and sheer laziness, for starters. Then there were all the generations of ancestors who died of various maladies and sickly constitutions. No one was holding their breath for his recovery.

But my boy knew, of course. So he tossed on a cloak, grabbed up a bottle of his tonic (he'd already made a batch of the nasty stuff for just such an occasion) and rushed to the manor. I followed him, curious to see how he played this out. It was a purely recreational visit in this case; I would not be called upon to do my business anytime soon.

He adjusted his cloak at the door, shadowing his face in the depths of its hood for a flair of intrigue, and knocked. A servant opened it and stared at him. "I am a Wizard First Order," my boy said in a deep voice, presenting the tonic with a flourish. "I have seen into the future and I know all." He paused dramatically. "If the baron will drink this tonic, he will live. If not"—my boy shook his head sadly—"nothing can be done."

The servant looked down at the bottle. Everyone knew how superstitious the baron was and how angry he would be at a servant who ignored such a pronouncement. The servant grabbed the bottle from my boy's hand and slammed the door. I grinned, so proud. My boy had finally found the perfect mark.

Not surprisingly, the baron recovered, and it didn't take long for the rumors to run abroad that a mysterious wizard had provided the elixir that saved him. The next time someone fell ill, my boy was there.

People began to notice.

Then they began to call on him.

I watched it all, standing near all those sickbeds, enjoying my godson's rise to fame and fortune. Amazing. Brilliant. Sneaky too, which seemed appropriate for my godchild.

Unfortunately, fame and fortune have a way of going to your head. He kept wanting more. Seeing his rise and his wants, I wondered what would *ever* be enough. A thought began to form in my head. Maybe he didn't know what he wanted after all. Maybe I could help him find what he was looking for.

Then came the day that the king fell ill. My boy was desperate to be called to the case. Surely this would satisfy his need.

And because of my boy's fame, his hopes were fulfilled. A messenger appeared on his door one day, summoning him to the palace.

I remember the moment he came out of the burning room, having just gone in to see the king's candle. I knew, of course. I always knew. Every candle I'd ever made. I knew how long it would burn.

I knew the king was destined for death.

The boy came out of that room, face pale, steps slow. How do you prepare to tell a king he is going to die?

I said nothing, but silently followed him to the palace. It was Death's job, after all, not just to make the candles but to witness the end.

Imagine my surprise, then, when he didn't offer the tragic news.

"You'll be well quite soon," he said confidently, "as long as you drink my tonic."

I stared at him aghast. He carefully did not look at me as he administered his medicine. I promptly left to check my candles.

The king's was burning bright and long. What had the boy done? He'd sneaked in and added to the king's wick! I could see the telltale signs of new dipping, the way the wax hadn't fully hardened around the addition. The work was impressive. Now the king was meant to die of old age, many years into the future.

I chuckled. He was quick and sneaky, but I wasn't about to tell him I was impressed. When he finally slinked in, face downcast as if he was ashamed—as if I couldn't see the satisfied gleam in his eye—I gave him a stern lecture.

"I'm sorry, but I just couldn't let him die," he said at the end of it, looking up at me with his best *I'm your godson, don't be mad* face. "He's the *king*, after all."

I rolled my eyes. "Don't bother with the fake apologies. This had better not happen again," I told him. "Or else..."

I let that threat hang in the air, since it seemed unnecessary to finish it. I'm Death, after all. Pretty much a one-trick pony.

He nodded and gave me a hug, which surprised me speechless. No one hugs Death.

But as luck would have it, the princess got sick just a month later, and my boy was immediately called in to examine her. Of course, I knew her disease was coming. And I knew her intended end. Hadn't I watched her candle slowly burn down for years?

My poor boy was just going to have to accept that sometimes I come at the least convenient moments.

We stood at the young woman's deathbed, surrounded by the grave faces of those who had loved and served her. I think they could sense me there, but since my boy was there too, they hoped the feeling was wrong. He looked down at her. She was quite lovely, this girl. A shame she should go so early, but that's just the way things are sometimes.

My boy opened his mouth to pronounce her fate. He glanced furtively at me, then, to my astonishment, he pulled out a flask of his tonic. "You called on me just in time," he said. "She is in terrible danger, but if she takes this tonic, she will yet live."

I guess I shouldn't have been surprised (and some part of me wasn't) as I stood there watching the boy cheat me again—cheating *Death*! I flew back to my shop, and there it was, the princess's candle, strong and tall and burning bright.

I shook my head and chuckled, finally coming to a conclusion I had begun to lean toward years ago.

This time he was obviously more nervous when he appeared at my door. And well he should have been.

"Come in," I told him.

He entered slowly. "I had to do it," he began. "It was the princess! They offered me—"

"Tut tut," I said, shushing him. "Fool me once, shame on you. Fool me twice... well, I should have known. But none of that matters. What matters is that twice you have used your knowledge against me. The knowledge that I gave you."

He hung his head.

"It's proof," I said.

He looked up, a puzzled expression crossing his face. "Proof of what?"

This was where we'd been heading all along, I realized, from the moment that he'd told me his dreams. "Proof that you're ready to take over my job."

His mouth gaped. "What?"

"You said you wanted fame and fortune. Fortune you have received, but you still wanted more. Fame you have received, but you *still* wanted more. My boy, you haven't understood. All these years, you thought you wanted fame and fortune, but that's not your true dream. Tricking people and taking their money will never satisfy you."

He continued to stare.

"Your name, spoken with awe, by all who speak it. That's what you said. Trust me," I said. "As me, you will have that. And what's more—you'll have meaning." I shrugged. "Okay, it's not *all* great. People really don't like you when you're Death. But trust me, there are moments that make it worth it." I smiled at him. "I got to be your godfather, after all."

He didn't immediately answer. He only clenched his jaw in silence, thinking. "How does it work?" he asked.

Goodness, that boy and his questions.

I went to the little shelf with the violet burning candle. "You asked me once," I said, "whose candle this was. I suspect you figured it out." I held it up for him to see. "This is me." I walked to a shelf I had hidden in a little alcove where I knew he would never find it (though I'm sure he looked more than once). "And this"—I picked up a candle—"is you."

I held them up for him to see and waited as the thoughts flitted through his mind. I could do this against his will, of course—that was how *I* had been made Death—but it didn't seem like the godfatherly sort of thing to do. And I *had* tried to be a good godfather.

Moments passed. Eternities passed. These sorts of things don't matter to Death.

Finally he took a breath and nodded. I was right. He would make a good Death.

I tilted my candle toward his flame, and for the first time in centuries, my wax began to melt. It dripped into his flame and sizzled, but instead of dissipating, it began to clump onto his candle. His flame began to change color, to darken. Mine became brighter, purer. By the time I had finished, our candles were both completely transformed. I did not look at mine too closely. After all these years of knowledge, I thought I'd rather not know.

"You are Death now," I told him. "Someday you'll have an apprentice too. You'll know when you find the right one. Didn't I know it, after all? You with all your questions and curiosity and terrible sneakiness?"

He chuckled, and there was something strange in his voice that had never been there before. It made me shiver, against my will. This was my boy, yes, but now he was Death too, and the mortal in me felt it.

"You'll train him—or maybe her." I had met some girls who probably would have made excellent Deaths. "Then you can finish out your mortal days."

"What about you?" he asked.

I shrugged. "I'm human now. I think maybe I'll go be the real candlemaker I used to be. I seem to recall I was rather good at it." I turned toward the door.

He reached out. "But when will I see you again?"

I laughed and pointed to the candle that once was Death's. "You tell me." I shook my head quickly. "On second thought"—I smiled—"don't."

Breadcrumbs

EVERY DAY WAS MUCH the same for Gretel. She awoke, suddenly, to a piercing scream echoing through her nightmares, accompanied by the smell of gingerbread. She startled from bed, her heart pounding. She told herself that it was just a dream, but that was a lie.

To push the memories from her mind, she rose, headed down the narrow stairway into the kitchen, and began her day's work. She cooked porridge for breakfast over a little stove, made up frybreads in a pot. The oven stood neglected, used only when absolutely necessary; Gretel had no taste for baking and ovens.

She worked until the rest of the household awoke. Her father always came downstairs next, already fully dressed, ready to slip out and away as soon as possible. It had been over five years since her stepmother's death, since Gretel and Hansel had returned from the forest, but her father was still the tiny man he'd been then.

Gretel often wondered if it was the memory of his guilt that kept him from looking her in the eye when he mumbled his "Good morning" and scurried to work. Had that one small choice—his choice to abandon his children—shaped everyone and everything in Gretel's life?

When Hansel came down from his bedroom, though, she doubted it. "Hello, dear sister," he'd say jubilantly, planting a quick peck on her cheek. "I think I shall go out today to try to bag a stag." Or maybe, "I'm off to spear a deer." When he'd laugh at his own rhyme, Gretel couldn't help but laugh with him. Hansel was what he had always been—funny and likable and full of plans. He spent his days hunting and making friends in the nearest town and doing who knew what else. The terror of those days in the gingerbread house in the forest hadn't cast their shadow on him.

Maybe if his had been the hands that pushed. Maybe then he would still hear the witch's screams in his nightmares.

Gretel would stir whatever she was preparing on the stove that day, whisking the sounds out of her brain. Hansel would grab some frybreads from the table and head out the door into the forest. She wondered how he could do that, walk into the woods so nonchalantly. But she noticed he never headed the direction they'd taken that day so long ago, and he always followed the signs he had cut into the trees. Notches in wood don't disappear like breadcrumbs.

With the men gone, Gretel would be mercifully alone again. She did not go into town often, as they did. The townsfolk all knew her family—they had even known her stepmother—but no one knew what had happened those months when Gretel and Hansel had disappeared. Since no one knew the truth of her family's story, they could not know the truth of her. And because they did not know her truth, everything felt like a lie.

Her housework, on the other hand, was dependable, understood. She swept, sewed, gathered vegetables from their little garden plot. Quiet, peaceful work she could relax into. Each activity was automatic, her hands and fingers going through the motions she'd set for them and repeated daily through the years. That way she could set her mind adrift, floating on a sea of soothing nothingness until the men came home at night and she was wrenched back into the world.

It had been five years. Surely life should have gotten better by now. And some days it was. Some days the supper conversation was gentle, or laughing, or loving, full of the events of the day and thoughts of the future—but then she would remember.

She remembered the blankness in their father's eyes when he and their stepmother took them into the woods to die. She remembered how he wouldn't lift a hand to save his own children. She remembered the fear when she and Hansel knew they were lost, how their breadcrumb path had been eaten away by birds they hadn't thought to plan for. The hope when they saw the gingerbread cottage in the forest. How that hope turned to horror, days and nights and weeks and months of it, ending in the final horror of the witch's burning flesh.

Remembering, she would rise from the table, politely excuse herself to her room, and scream her rage and despair into her pillow.

Such was every day for Gretel, an endless round of remembering and forgetting and restlessness and stillness.

She couldn't say exactly when she decided to leave. It was like baking—there was no single moment when a loaf went from dough to bread, it was simply a process of time and heat. Maybe it was watching her father slink off to work every day, never meeting her eyes, yet never seeking forgiveness. Maybe it was the way Hansel laughed when she shuddered suddenly as the oven door caught her gaze. Maybe it was the slow-burning realization that they could all easily spend the next ten years together as they had spent the last five, nothing changing. She was nearly seventeen now; most of the girls in town were betrothed or married, heading out to new lives and worlds. They were not her friends, and she did not envy them, but maybe a seed of change breezed past them and settled in her soul.

Whatever the reason, Gretel lay awake in bed late one night, staring at the rafters, realizing she could not stay in this place another day. She'd been waiting for something to magically change, as it always did in the fairy tales from her childhood. She could barely remember those tales from when her real mother was still alive, filling her head with stories of wonder and filling her heart with love. Planting dreams of happy endings.

But real life wasn't that way. Yes, there were the villains—she'd met them, after all—but no fairy godmother was ever going to appear just because Gretel was good and kind and hardworking. No djinn would emerge from a bottle and offer her heart's desire. And maybe that was because she too was a villain, because she had blood and ashes on her hands, but she didn't care anymore. If change wouldn't come by itself, she would bring the change.

She woke the next morning to a scream in her mind. She curled in on herself, for a moment sucked into the darkness of reliving that sound. It's over now, she remembered, and she opened her eyes to look around her bedroom, smooth her hands across her worn coverlet, reminding herself where she was. And where she would never be again. She brushed away hot tears. She would not let those memories conquer her any longer. She rose from bed and went through the usual morning routines, but her heart pounded with a new sensation, a precarious sort of excitement.

After the men had left for the day, she picked up the knapsack she'd already packed, placed a dagger in its sheath around her waist, left a note of farewell for Hansel and her father, and headed for the door.

She pushed it open and gazed out into the woods.

Don't think, just go.

But where? She rarely traveled and never alone. She didn't know where to go, though a tiny, insistent voice inside told her that no matter where she went, there was one place she must return to before she could start anew.

If she followed the path from her home, she would arrive in town and eventually at the carpenter's shop where her father worked. She could tell him goodbye. She doubted he would stop her, but if she went that way, she feared she might stop herself. If instead she turned left, stepping off the path, she would head in the direction of the gingerbread house. If she turned right, every step would take her farther away from it.

Fear told her to take any path but toward that little house, but the voice inside spoke louder. What good was it to leave behind one nightmare only to take another with you? She took a deep breath and turned left. She did not look back. She would not be dropping breadcrumbs this time.

Gretel walked a steady pace now across the soft sponge of the mossy forest floor. She breathed in the crisp air of the forest. The sun was high overhead, but the ground was still cool in the dappled shadows of the leaves. The woods did not frighten in reality as they had in her memory; the trees were still large, but they didn't loom.

Even knowing where she was headed did not fill her with the terror she'd expected. It was as if, with every step away from her old life, something new rose within her, something green and growing and fragile, easily crushed but straining into life.

An hour passed, then two and three, and Gretel began to finally feel an uneasy sense of familiarity. It came with the breeze, and at first she didn't recognize its scent. But then it wafted past again, and she knew it: the tang of molasses and ginger. Her steps slowed as the tension she'd been releasing returned in full, filling her stomach with nausea. For the first time she looked back, *away*. It wasn't too late to turn another direction.

She stopped and took a deeper breath, letting the scent fill her nose and her lungs, clinging to a nearby tree trunk to keep herself from running. She closed her eyes, waiting for the terror to lull, then pushed forward. Only another minute passed before she saw her living nightmare at a distance through the trees.

In a small clearing stood the little brown house. White icing in cheerful scallops ran around the windows, under the eaves, across every shingle of the pitched roof. Around the foot of the walls brightly colored gumdrops, red, yellow, green, blue, sat in neat rows like a sweet, sticky garden. The windows were delicately tinted poured sugar, sheets so thin she knew they let light into the house yet still strong enough to keep out the wind. The walls, of course, were gingerbread. The whole cottage seemed perfectly preserved, exactly as she had last seen it those years ago.

Gretel's stomach clenched, and the blood pounded strangely through her veins. Her head was light, but her feet felt glued to the ground. Surely time should have decayed such a confection. Surely it should have been a ruin by now.

Surely, Gretel tried to tell herself, the witch was not still alive and tending to her home.

Gretel's stomach squeezed again, and this time she dropped to her knees to retch up the remains of her breakfast into the leaves and dirt. When she was through, she wiped her mouth and forced herself to look again. She noticed other details this time. The striped candy shutters, the poofs of divinity lining the walkway, everything exactly as she had tried to forget.

In the middle of the cottage stood the only element that could not be consumed: a tall stone chimney, rising up like a monument. Though it was indoors, Gretel could see its base clearly in memory—an oven door, wide enough to admit the entire body of a child. Or a witch.

She watched that chimney, holding her breath, waiting to see the telltale smoke of a burning fire, but the air was still. Nothing stirred in or around the house, but Gretel didn't trust its appearance. Truth be told, she hadn't trusted that house the first time she saw it either, but hunger and fear had driven her to ignore her instincts.

She would not make the same mistake this time.

So she stood longer, watching the house from a distance, waiting for signs of activity. Minutes passed, then hours. In the stillness of watching, every sound became amplified. A leaf falling to the ground crackled as it landed. The rustle of the breeze through the tree branches thundered. She noticed, however, that no animals chittered nearby, no birds called in this area. She shivered with more than the chill of the wind.

Maybe the cottage truly had been abandoned, and only its lingering magic preserved it. Nothing had changed in hours. Nothing had changed in five years. Maybe nothing would ever change here. Maybe it was time to move on. She tried to convince herself that she was being practical, not cowardly, as she turned her back to the house, studiously ignoring it as she picked up her knapsack and fetched a snack to settle her uneasy stomach.

In the stillness, she heard a distinct *snap*.

She twisted back to face the house and saw, with horror, that a man had walked out of the forest and was standing there. The snapping sound came from a hand-sized chunk of gingerbread that he'd broken from the eaves.

"Don't eat that!" she shouted, rushing from her hiding place toward him. She reached the man and swatted his gingerbread to the ground, stomping it to pieces.

He stared at her, eyes wide, then glanced at the crumbled remains at his feet. "Why not?" he asked.

Gretel panted from the exertion of the dash and the sudden terror that had flooded her. "Believe me... you don't want it. You shouldn't come here." She grabbed his hand and tried to pull him back into the safety of the trees.

The man resisted. Gretel hesitated, torn between saving herself from the witch and trying to save the foolish man as well.

"I've come here before," he said, and his voice had gone soft, the way you talk to a wild creature. "It's safe. It's... peaceful, even. Not even the animals come near."

Peaceful. Gretel's stare darted to the house. She could not think of this place as peaceful. She looked at the man again. He was younger than she'd first thought, perhaps only a few years her elder. Handsome, in a gentle way, with dark hair and the muscles of a woodsman. But the expression in his brown eyes suggested sorrow and pain that was fresh. "You find *peace* here?"

"I know the house is a little strange. It's in perfect condition, and the gingerbread grows back." He shrugged and gazed out into the distance, seeing things she couldn't. "But there are worse things than strange."

Gretel's hands were still shaking with the remains of terror, but she realized how foolish she seemed. Of course the witch was gone. Of course nothing bad would happen from eating the gingerbread now, but she hadn't been able to think logically when she saw that piece of gingerbread in his hand. "You're right, I'm sorry. I just…"

"What did you *think* would happen?" he asked, returning his gaze to her.

She shook her head. "Nothing, nothing. I apologize. I overreacted." Now that the moment had passed, she felt a new fear. She wasn't sure about trusting a stranger in the woods. She carefully reached for her dagger and drew it from its sheath.

"I've never seen anyone else here before," he said, watching her cautiously. "I didn't think anyone else even knew it existed."

"I haven't been here for five years."

"And why are you here now?" He kept his eyes on her dagger.

Gretel's inner voice, the one she could sometimes hear when the pain was quiet, suggested that at this moment he was not the dangerous one. She lowered her dagger but did not put it away. "That is my business."

He shrugged. "Fair enough." He gestured toward her dagger. "I'm not going to harm you. I only came here to think." Then he pointed to a long log bench near the edge of the clearing. "Do you mind if I sit?"

Gretel shook her head and gestured an invitation.

"I made that bench. Decided if I was going to keep coming here, I needed a spot to sit." Sorrow appeared in his eyes again, but he said nothing more.

In spite of herself, Gretel was curious. She followed him and sat on the bench too, but as far from him as she could. She leaned back. "It's comfortable."

"Yes. A must for thinking." He stared out into the woods while his hand moved to touch a bag at his side. Gretel tightened her grip on her dagger, but he didn't seem to notice. He drew a wooden box from the bag, about the size of a round of bread. His finger traced a pattern painted on it, a strange shape like a red waterskin with several drinking spouts. It looked familiar, but she couldn't place it. "She wanted me to be a murderer," he said, almost to himself.

"I am already a murderer," she responded, surprised into honesty as she stared at the chimney that held both an oven and a grave.

He looked at her, snapped briefly out of his thoughts. He didn't seem afraid. "Really?"

She nodded once. "Here, in this place. I killed to save my life and the life of my brother."

A moment of silence, then, "Tell me," he said.

Only once had she ever told even part of this tale, to her father, the night that she and Hansel had returned from the forest. Since then she'd held it close and guarded it in her heart, afraid of what the telling would do to her, of how the hearer would react. Yet here, in the shadow of the gingerbread house, with a stranger her heart told her she could trust—here it flowed from her lips.

The young man listened as the words poured from her, revealing each little morsel of the world she had lived in every day of her life since they'd come home—the pain at her father's betrayal and cowardice, the fierce but terrifying relief of the witch's death and the news of her stepmother's death as well. The unbearable guilt of killing, no matter how justified.

She cast out the words, the feelings, with an energy that at first made her burn with their power. She had never said these words this way before, with the freedom to tell the truth. Who cared what this stranger thought, this stranger whose story held darkness too? If once she could say it all, without care to soften the words, to hide the scars, who knew what might happen?

She told him of the unchanging years of forcing herself into numbness, of hiding from everyone—her family, the townspeople, and especially herself. The more she told, the more the rage quieted, the more she found relief in the words. They slowed, they soothed her. They reformed themselves almost with a will of their own. They began to feel like a different story altogether. A story where she wasn't the villain any longer. She wasn't the victim. She was just Gretel, someone new, someone transformed, someone—maybe—free.

She knew, instinctively, that it was a story she would have to tell herself again and again. But for the first time it existed, and *that* felt like the budding of hope.

Finally she fell silent, and the two of them stared ahead into the beginnings of dusk falling over the house.

"You are not a murderer," he said firmly. When she didn't respond, he continued. "You did it to save yourself and your brother. No one can call that murder." He pointed to the house. "Think of all the other children you may have saved too. Who knows how many she would have killed."

She bit her lip in thought. "I hadn't thought of them. Maybe I did save them." She smiled, and the idea of those children, safe now, took root in her soul. She breathed deeply—her first unfettered breath in five years—and though the scent of spices on the air called to her fears, she didn't let them overwhelm her.

"I had never told anyone all of this." She tilted her head to the side. "I owe you much. I think maybe more than I can repay."

He opened his mouth to reply, but she waved her hand to stop him.

"No, I know you weren't looking for payment, but I owe you nonetheless. I can't do much, but I *can* do one thing, the same thing you did for me." She turned to face him fully. "Tell me your story."

He still held the box in his hands, and now he opened it. Within it lay a darkened, bloody object that matched the picture on the box—a heart; that was why she recognized it. She looked into his eyes, hers widening. "I thought you said you were only *meant* to be a murderer."

Quickly he shook his head. "No, no, it's not human. It's a pig's heart. But I must take it to my queen and pretend it is human, or she will hunt the owner of the heart she really wants."

The young man's tale was nearly as mad as her own. He told of a coldhearted queen in the neighboring kingdom who wanted to be the most beautiful woman in the land. He told of a girl who threatened that beauty and of the queen's command to take the young woman into the forest and kill her. Gretel shuddered. She wondered, would it be better to be killed outright in the forest or, as Gretel had been, merely left to die?

Either way, the man couldn't do it. He'd let the girl go, showing her a way to safety. He'd slaughtered a pig and taken its heart. He was on his way back to deceive the queen.

"I loved her," he said softly, closing the lid on the heart.

"The girl?" she asked.

He shook his head. "No. The queen."

The words rang for a moment in silence.

"I loved her from afar of course. For too long I loved her. I tried to pretend she wasn't as she seemed. I came out here to pretend, to forget, so I could go back and be her servant again." He laughed without mirth. "But I can't pretend anymore."

She knew too well that pain.

He shrugged, trying to lighten the mood. "My mother was right when she told me I should acquire better taste in women."

Gretel smiled. "Next time pick someone who doesn't like to kill." She blushed and looked away.

"I'll do that." He chuckled ruefully.

"You saved a child without having to kill anyone. I envy you that."

He reached his hand out to comfort her but pulled back.

"If your queen finds out you tricked her, she'll kill you."

He nodded. "Yes."

"Run away."

He hesitated a moment, staring into the distance. "Maybe."

"Leave. Start somewhere else," Gretel urged, uncertain why her throat tightened at the thought of his danger. "You owe her nothing."

"No, but I owe the girl. I have to at least deliver the heart. Then? Then we'll see."

The noisy rustle of a sudden gust of wind through the trees broke the spell woven by the mutual telling of tales, and they both looked around for what seemed like the first time in hours. Darkness was falling quickly now.

"I must be on my way back," the man said, reluctantly.

She rose. "I'll be going too."

He looked straight into her eyes. "Maybe we'll meet in the woods again someday."

"Maybe. On a better day for us both."

"This day has turned out far better than I expected when it began." He stretched out his hand to take hers in a gentle grip. "Thank you, Gretel."

What could she say to this man to whom she had broken her silence? She had said so much already. In the end she could only nod, her throat clogged with emotion. He turned away, and she watched him go, following his shape through the forest until he was beyond her sight.

A moment later, she looked toward the house. She had lied; she wasn't going anywhere yet. There was one thing left to do here.

She steeled herself and walked to the door.

Her fingers trembled as she reached toward the door latch. She sucked in a breath, and the scent of sugar and cinnamon and nutmeg overpowered her senses and dragged her away again, back to that time in the gingerbread house, when she wondered every day if she would once again be able to convince the witch that Hansel was too thin to eat for supper.

She shuddered, then shook her head to dislodge the memory. That's all it was, a memory. The house held no power any longer, no witch to harm her. Still she hesitated, her fingers a breath away from the latch. She swallowed and tried to breathe through her mouth, but even then the scent, so strong this close to the house, threatened to pull her under again.

She drew back. She could see the inside of the house in her memory. The last light of dusk filtering through the sugared window panes tinged the room blue and green and red. The witch's chair stood in the corner with a bag of knitting. The stove, the shelves, the door to the witch's bedroom, she saw them all in her mind. And there, in the center of the room, the oven that had filled her nightmares for so many nights.

The recollection made her dizzy. She pressed her hands against the smooth gingerbread doorpost to keep herself from falling. She couldn't go in. Not tonight. This day had swept away so much of the nightmare, and yet so much remained.

It didn't matter. This house was just a house. Going inside it was not some magic spell that would solve all her problems. She could do that herself. She could leave here and move on.

One day, someday soon maybe, she'd wake to the sounds of birds chirping a morning greeting instead of vivid, echoing nightmare screams. One day she wouldn't fill every moment with tasks deliberately chosen to make her forget. Maybe then she'd come back and step into the gingerbread rooms without fear. Maybe she'd come back and sit on the log bench to wait for a thoughtful stranger to appear. Maybe she'd offer him a loaf of bread and they'd sit in the sunshine and talk and laugh and when the meal was done she'd break off a piece of gingerbread for dessert.

Or maybe she wouldn't.

Gretel turned away from the house, facing the darkening woods. What would she do next? She'd focused so long on forgetting that she almost didn't know there was anything else.

But now a memory rose up from her childhood, like a tiny curl of leaf unfurling from a seed long lost in the ground. She'd wanted to travel the world, back then, when she didn't know how much danger the world could hold. She'd wanted to see lakes and mountains and caves, meet dwarves and fairies, find out if unicorns were real.

She'd buried that dream under gingerbread nightmares, but now bits of the nightmares crumbled and fell away as the dream rose again within her, struggling out into the light. Gretel touched her dream gently, brushing gingerbread crumbs from its leaves. So delicate, but with strength in its roots.

She settled her knapsack firmly on her shoulder, picked up the sprout of a new dream, and headed down an unknown path into the woods. The gingerbread house faded into the distance behind her.

The Cinderella Plan

I WATCHED AS THE archduke approached, gingerly carrying a ridiculously impractical glass slipper across the room. Soon he would ask me to try it on. This was my moment. Feigning clumsiness as he presented it to me, I jostled his wrist and gasped as the slipper crashed to the floor.

At first he only stared in shock at the scattered shards, but then he began to weep. Poor man. He'd surely been through a lot as the archduke to this particular royal family.

"Don't cry," I told him, reaching into my apron pocket. "I have the other one." His eyes darted to the shoe I held out, and he began to smile again.

Trust a man not to notice the glaring size difference between the original slipper and mine.

"Thank you for finding me!" I threw my arms around him and wailed. A little melodrama couldn't hurt. "I've missed my prince so desperately!"

He escorted me out to the carriage. And just like that, I was on my way to the palace and my betrothal.

I'd resisted my parents' suggested brides for years. The fiscal irresponsibility of the parties they dreamed of throwing for my nuptials was almost a greater deterrent than the brides themselves.

Almost.

Apparently my parents' only requirement for my wife was that she sport the latest hairstyle. A brain was unnecessary. And a bit of common sense was quite undesirable. They didn't want someone who would actually agree with my budgets and projections. At this rate, by the time the kingdom became mine, it would be destroyed.

As my parents increased the pressure to marry—increasing the costs of their wife-finding extravaganzas as well—I finally came up with a desperate plan. A fake mystery woman. A whirlwind romance. An impossibly tiny glass slipper that would never fit anyone.

I would gain months of peace if I could convince my parents I was heartbroken when the archduke couldn't find my true love.

Of course I wasn't the girl from the ball. She didn't exist. I was just a girl with a few unorthodox ideas, a penchant for eavesdropping on secret plans, and an unhealthy love of meddling. But no one listens to the ideas of an unimportant glassblower's niece, no matter how marvelous. As the prince's new fiancée, however, I had a chance.

Oh, he wouldn't be pleased at first (men always think their plans are the only way to do something), but I was exactly what he needed.

The herald approached my parents' thrones and announced, "The archduke has returned, victorious in his search for the slipper's owner!"

"What?" I sputtered. "He wasn't supposed to—" Mother shot me a surprised look. "I mean... I'm so thrilled he's back. I just thought the journey would take longer." I pasted on a smile of delight. "Bring her in!" Then I would decide how to get rid of the impostor. No gold digger was going to trick her way into marrying me.

I sallied into the throne room wearing last year's gown. The queen had looked excited when I entered, but now she cringed. I smiled. She'd change her mind soon enough. But first I had to convince the prince to hear me out.

"Darling! I feared we'd be parted forever." I ran to him and threw my arms around his neck—the perfect position for secret conversation. Plus it couldn't hurt to waft a little lilac scent over him.

"Who are you?" he hissed into my ear.

"Your fiancée, of course," I whispered back.

"Whatever you want, you're not getting it."

Straight to the point, then. "I want to help you. You've been going about things with your parents all wrong. Spreadsheets will never convince them to change."

"Oh? And what will?"

I smiled wickedly. "Fashion, my dear."

He pulled back, aghast. "Fashion?"

"Yes," I told him firmly. "Retro-minimalist fashion, to be exact. We're going to change the whole castle's economy—bring back all the dresses and breeches and stuff that's been sitting in the attic for starters."

He did not look impressed.

"I made some charts for you to look at," I added.

"You did?" He perked up. The prince couldn't resist a good chart.

"Yes. But first we have to convince them this is real."

"How?"

"Kiss me, of course." I winked.

Could her plan possibly work? She smiled warmly, and I thought it might be worth a try. I'd have to consult her charts to decide for sure, but maybe my fortunes—and my kingdom's—were turning around. So I leaned down to kiss my new ally. My new fiancée.

Now I just had to find out her name.

A Selection of Documents Related to the Incidents Occurring at the July 2025 Young Women Camp of the Forest Thicket 2nd Ward

AUTHOR'S NOTE:

This story is based in the very specific culture of The Church of Jesus Christ of Latter-day Saints. While the context of the story is specific to my church culture, I like to think that the ideas and themes are a little more universal. If, however, you are averse to stories that are overtly set within a religious tradition, you may want to skip this one.

Some terms/experiences that may be unfamiliar are loosely defined here: A ward is a local church congregation. A bishop is the pastor of a ward; other church titles include elder and president, along with positions like executive secretary and counselors. A meeting with the bishop often means you're getting a new assignment in the ward, known as a calling.

Members of the church often call each other brother and sister. The Young Women/YW organization is for girls ages 12 to 18, and they generally have weekly activities together, as well as a summer camp. Finally, a defining belief of our church is that all of us on earth are beloved children of divine Heavenly Parents—a king and a *queen—and we have the potential to become like them. In that sense, we're all kind of princes and princesses.*

Text conversation between Sister Beth Larsen and Brother Alvin Schmidt of the Forest Thicket 2nd Ward, 28 March

Hi, Sis Larsen. Can you meet with Bishop Reynolds this Sunday just before church?

...

...

Yes.

Great, see you then.

Text conversation between Beth Larsen and her husband, Erick Larsen, two minutes later

Ummm, just got a message from the exec sec to meet with the bishop.

> Uh oh.

Yeah.

> You're gonna do great, whatever it is.

> If you bring up that Eyring quote again, I will reach through this phone and strangle you.

> Then I will definitely NOT remind you that God's gonna make up what we can't do. It's going to be okay. And I will definitely NOT remind you that Elder Eyring said that.

> *Sigh.* I know. Go forward with faith and all that. I just hope it's not… well, never mind, that's the kind of thing you never say/write out loud.

> Ha! True. You can do it. I love you and you will figure this out.

Agenda for handover meeting between Sister Tamara Muller, former Young Women president, and Sister Beth Larsen, new Young Women president, in the Forest Thicket 2nd Ward, 4 May

*Sister Larsen's notes marked in italics; doodles and exclamation points redacted

- Opening prayer: Sister Larsen

- Spiritual thought: Sister Muller
  "There will be times when you will feel overwhelmed. There will be times when you will feel inadequate. Well, you are inadequate to represent God with your own abilities, but you will be magnified, and you do not work alone." (by Elder Eyring)

Seriously, Elder Eyring again! Is this a sign?

- Discussion of individual Young Women:

    - Lauren: *seventh child; very handy, pretty much spins straw into gold*

    - Chiara: *parents forgot to invite godmother to name/blessing, so she's got a mysterious curse; sleeps a lot; really likes to admire herself*

    - Maya: *father died a year ago; stepmother and stepsisters friendly so far, but definitely keep an eye on that*

    - Eliza: *no known angry relatives; always at church; plays baseball and volleyball*

- Overview of Young Women activities for May: *(Activities are brainstormed by girls and they choose who will lead what activity)*

    - Handwork and crafting, Lauren—girls will be learning how to embroider magical tablecloths, how to gather thistles without injury, and basic construction techniques for flying carpets

- Animal husbandry, Maya—how to talk to them, ethics of how to interact *(Stuff like making friends, not asking them to do your homework, but maybe asking for help with chores? Must think about this one)*

- Pedicure night, Chiara—bring lots of glittery nail polish *(Yay! Haven't done my nails in forever)*

• Young Women Camp this year:

- Dates and location are set: 21–25 July, on the edge of the Dark Forest, per tradition

- Theme still to be chosen

- Activities/devotionals/food still to be chosen

- Cautions related to the Dark Forest and our girls:

Humans—good or bad—masquerading as bears, deer, foxes, wolves, moose, fish, mice, frogs, spiders

Humans—good or bad—hiding in ponds, trees, buckets, shadows

Remember to put out milk for brownies (not the food brownies, though maybe put those on the menu?)

Pixies too—annoying like brownies (again, not the food), but mostly harmless; can't be avoided, only endured

Some sort of vague rumor about a dark presence, pretty sure I heard the same rumor when I was in YW

Ummm, she mentioned a couple other things, but I sort of zoned out for a minute

• Additional notes:
Yikes, there's like a million things that could go wrong here.

> *We've gotta be violating some sort of worker safety laws, right? Whose idea was it to have Young Women camp right next to the Dark Forest?*

- Final thoughts and thank you: Sister Muller
  Lots of thanks, cheerleading, you can do it, yada yada

- Closing prayer: Sister Larsen

Journal entry of Beth Larsen, 5 May

Absolutely freaking out. Had the handover meeting with Sis. Muller today, and I was actually feeling okay about things. Sure, there's a lot of needs in a ward like this, so close to the Dark Forest. I knew there would probably be some curses to deal with, some fairies to look out for, that sort of thing. But Sis. Muller gave me lots of good info, and I was thinking, "Okay, I can do this."

And then she mentioned Young Women Camp.

Young. Women. Camp.

Is it maybe not too late to back out? Because camping and bugs and sleeping on rocks and lighting fires in pits and peeing in a hole? No thank you.

And then the worst part: The planning and the theme and the relating to the girls and the trying to be cool enough that they like me but bossy enough that they listen to me. I'm just not sure I can handle this. Ugh.

Announcement posted by Sister Beth Larsen in Forest Thicket 2nd Ward Discord group, 6 May

SAVE THE DATE!

21–25 July

Young Women Camp this year is going to be SO MUCH FUN!

Get ready for good fun, good food, friendships, and testimony building!!!

Young Women, I am so excited to get to spend this week with you out in the woods and having fun and learning together! I really hope you can come!!!!

Compiled excerpts from Young Women presidency meeting agendas, focusing on theme selection, May and June

Sister Larsen's notes marked in italics; some exclamation points redacted

In attendance:
- Beth Larsen, president
- Charlotte Neumann, 1st counselor
- No 2nd counselor or secretary called

Purpose of theme:

- To help the Young Women know that they are needed, loved, and important to their Heavenly Parents

- To establish a main topic for devotionals and other spiritual activities

Theme ideas:
- Slaying Dragons: *no! no dragons!*

- Be Your Own Kind of Beautiful: *very 1980s*

- Looking in the Mirror, Seeing You're Beautiful: *ugh, so wordy*

- Who Do You See in the Mirror?: *giving creepy horror flick vibes*

- We Are Family: *I appreciate the Sister Sledge ref, but will anyone else?*

- Trees in a Forest: *just because we'll be in a forest doesn't mean we're trees*

- Daughters of a King: *ooh, getting warmer maybe? it's got importance in it...*

- Princesses among Ogres: *nope, too "us against them"*

- Don't Be a Troll: *ha! but no*

- Divine Princesses: *yes. Yes! YES!!!!!!!!!!!!!*

Announcement posted by Sister Beth Larsen in Forest Thicket 2nd Ward Discord group, 5 July

WE ARE ALL DIVINE PRINCESSES!

Young Women: This is your friendly reminder that if you haven't turned in your camp permission form, do it soon!

Parents: This is your friendly reminder to pester your daughters!

It's going to be a great week of learning about our divine missions as daughters of Heavenly Parents. Also, there's going to be fun and games and lots of food. :)

Beth Larsen's to-do list, scrawled on sticky note, 20 July; found stuck to the bottom of a stack of miscellaneous papers, 12 August

> Remember to pack:
> - Extra rope for macrame
> - Big wooden stirring spoon

Secret Sister note from [redacted] to Eliza F., attached to a candy bar, 22 July

> Hi, Eliza. Your Secret Sister thinks you're really 100 Grand! You're so nice. Keep smiling!

Entry from Maya P.'s journal, 23 July

We're supposed to be out here communing with nature and trying to build our spirits and stuff, but I'm just trying to avoid all the frogs. Because ick. I really hate frogs. I like talking to animals usually, just not frogs. Ick again. Fortunately, I've climbed up into a low branch of a tree, so I'm too high off the ground for them to reach me.

Camp has been good so far. We came up with a camp cheer and we've been singing songs and doing cheesy talent skits and stuff. I really like the singing part, but they keep telling me I have to sing quieter because I attract the wildlife. I sometimes think the animal thing isn't all that great.

Yesterday during the sunrise hike a swarm of pixies flew in and kinda messed everything up. They stole all our hairbrushes and hid them somewhere, and they piled everyone's socks in the fire pit. So now we all have socks that smell like smoke. Which is maybe better than Chiara's smelled after she accidentally stepped in wyvern poo yesterday. Ew. So I guess the pixies were a blessing.

The food has been good, but Sis. Larsen forgot to bring a spoon to stir last night's stew, so we had to find a big ole stick to stir it with, and then Lauren and Chiara started cackling and pretending to be witches stirring a potion, but apparently they actually did have some magic because the stew started glowing green and Sis. Larsen said it probably wasn't safe to eat anymore, so we just had sandwiches instead, which was okay, and then we also had really yummy lava cake for dessert.

Oh, we just got the warning bell to come back. I think we're doing macrame next. I'll try to write more tomorrow.

Entry from Chiara G.'s journal, 24 July

Okay, whoa. Whoa!!! Last night was insane! So I'm not exactly sure what happened, because I slept through the first part and then I woke up soooo sore, like someone had dropped a moose on my ribs or something. But I woke up just in time to use my socks, and no one better complain about them ever again. Also, I sacrificed my mirror, which I'm really gonna miss. My hair is a disaster this morning.

Anyway, they've been all hush-hushy about it, so I'm not sure why that prince was here, but I think he was trying to cart one of us off to be his princess! SO scary! (Even if he was kinda hot.) But we're all okay now, except the leaders have taken us to go journal in the woods while they take turns talking to the police. I am absolutely dying to find out what actually happened, though, so I'm gonna cut this journaling short and go snoop.

Excerpt of police interview between Officer James Trenton and Charlotte Neumann

CN: [yawning] Sorry, I'm just a little tired. It was a long night.

OT: I understand, that's what we're here to talk about. Can you help me out? Explain what happened. All I have right now is a prince in a mirror, and he's trying to claim immunity, says he's a diplomat from across the forest and this is all just a mix-up.

CN: Well, that's a crock of wyvern dung.

OT: Yes, I have my suspicions about his true identity, but I need information from you and Ms. Larsen first.

CN: I'm not sure where to start.

OT: How about you start with the apples.

CN: [nodding] Right, that's good. Well, yesterday afternoon we took all the girls out to the forest to do a little bit of journal writing and reflection. I thought the camp was attended the whole time, but poor Brother Acker had food poisoning, so he spent a lot of that time lying in bed switching back and forth between ferret and human. It was apparently quite unpleasant.

OT: Magical food poisoning? How did that happen?

CN: It's kind of a funny story. He ate a potion the girls accidentally brewed the night before. We threw it out, but he was hungry and found it and, well, apparently it was a shapeshifting sort of a potion.

OT: We'll need to question him as well.

CN: No problem. The shapeshifting is slowing down, so as long as he doesn't stop on ferret [nervous chuckle], you should be able to talk to him soon.

OT: So he was indisposed, leaving the camp unsupervised?

CN: Yep. And I guess the prince—what did you say his name was?

OT: He says it's Kieran, but his ID looks fake to me. I'm checking some things out.

CN: Right. Anyway, he must have sneaked in and placed the apples in our dinner supplies. We were going to make apple cobbler. So we got back from the forest and didn't see anything wrong, and we started making dinner. But those apples... they were just so tempting...

OT: Ma'am? *Ma'am?*

CN: Oh, sorry. [blinking rapidly] Where was I?

OT: The apples.

CN: Right. In retrospect, there was obviously some sort of enchantment on them, since we were all so desperate to eat them. I sliced and sliced, but everyone kept snatching the slices. I almost chopped off Lauren's fingers! We didn't end up with enough left to actually make into cobbler. They were soooo good, juicy and sweet and mmm...

OT: *Ma'am?* What happened next?

CN: Whew, they sure packed a wallop. Even knowing what they are, I'm not sure I could resist one if it was sitting here right now. Anyway, we all ate them except Eliza. I honestly don't know how she resisted, but she's allergic to raw apple, so somehow she managed.

The apples had a sleeping spell on them, apparently, because we all got so tired we skipped the evening activities and went straight to bed. That's about all I know until I woke up to see Eliza in my tent shaking Sister Larsen and yelling at us to wake up.

Once we were finally awake, we went outside, and there was the prince, lying on the ground unconscious, with a big lump on the back of his head and tied up in blonde macrame.

OT: ... What?

CN: You know, macrame? It's that braided rope stuff you hang potted plants with?

OT: I know what macrame is, I'm just wondering why... blonde?

CN: Oh, the girls learned how to make rope this week with various material—torn up bedsheets, thistles, hair. We were just gonna learn macrame with regular rope, but Sister Larsen forgot to pack it so we had to make do, you know?

OT: Uh, sure.

CN: So anyway, she'd tied him up really well.

OT: And then you called the police and we came.

CN: Yep.

Excerpt of police interview between Officer James Trenton and Beth Larsen

BL: [crying] I can't believe how badly I messed this all up.
OT: [awkwardly patting her shoulder] It's going to be okay. All the girls are safe and uninjured...
BL: [incomprehensible mumbles]
OT: I really need a statement, if you're able to talk about it.
BL: [sniffing] Yes, um, okay. What do you need?
OT: How did this all start, from your perspective?
BL: It was that stupid theme! We thought and thought about it, and I could have just chosen a nice scriptural phrase or something simple like "Children of God," and everything would have been totally fine!
OT: That's not—
BL: But *no*, I had to overthink it. I just wanted the girls to know they're loved, you know? But then of course I chose the one theme that would attract some psychopathic stalker prince guy—and is he even really a prince?
OT: I—
BL: Because honestly, poisoning and then trying to drag off the girl you're interested in is *not* princely behavior. And then I couldn't just leave the theme on the announcements or maybe a little laminated reminder for the girls. No, I had to go completely overboard and plaster it across this huge banner that I hung up in camp saying "We are all divine princesses!"
OT: It's—

BL: Like some sort of neon sign screaming "Crazy princes, inquire within!" And now they're probably going to release me from my calling because I've made such a huge mess of things, and Elder Eyring was totally wrong, and I've just started getting to know the girls, and they're so sweet, and I just love them to pieces, and—[dissolves back into tears]

OT: ... Why don't I go get someone to sit with you. I can interview you later.

Excerpt of police interview between Officer James Trenton and Eliza F.

OT: I understand you didn't eat the apples.

EF: They were sooo tempting. But I'm allergic, and I kept hearing this little voice in my head saying I'd regret eating them. Wow, was that true.

OT: So when everyone else went to sleep, what did you do?

EF: I went to sleep too, but I'm a light sleeper. I think it was only maybe a couple hours later when I heard a sound in the camp. I thought it was a bear—they warned us a ton about not leaving any food out because bears might be attracted to it. We put everything in bear-proof containers, with locks just in case there was a bear who was actually a human. That happened to Maya's great aunt, only it was a stag, and—

OT: Thank you, I'm sure that's interesting, but tell me more about what happened then.

EF: So I heard the sound and I was still tired so I almost decided to go back to sleep. Nothing for me to do if it was a bear, right?

But the noise felt… creepy. I dunno, just wrong. I peeked my head outside the tent and saw this dark figure. Tall and dark, and he was leaving one of the tents, and I was so scared I didn't know what to do. I watched him go into another tent and I sneaked out of mine and looked around for a weapon. There was this Dutch oven that we hadn't used because we didn't make the apple cobbler. That seemed like a good idea, so I grabbed it. He was leaving the next tent by then, so I tried to hide behind one of the camp chairs.

OT: Did he see you?

EF: Nope. The chair was really small, so I was afraid he would, but I guess I've always been pretty good at being invisible, so he walked right past me into Chiara's tent. He left the zipper open, so I could see what he was doing. He bent down close to her and whispered something, then he kissed her! While she was asleep! That made me so mad I stopped thinking or being scared, I just rushed right at him and swung the Dutch oven at the back of his head.

OT: Swinging a Dutch oven? Those are pretty heavy, aren't they?

EF: [smiling] I play a lot of baseball, so I've got a pretty good arm.

OT: [smiling too] So what happened then?

EF: He fell forward, kind of flopped on Chiara. She's probably gonna have bruises. I rolled him off her and wrapped him up in Lauren's amazing macrame. Then I went to wake up Sister Larsen. It was really hard—I had to shake her and yell and stuff. Then she called you.

OT: And the prince woke before I could get here?

EF: Yeah, he wasn't asleep for long. He started whining that his head hurt and trying to call in his ravens to peck at us. Too bad for him, Lauren taught us all how to make sparkly friendship bracelets a couple weeks ago, and Maya is really good with animals. We gave the ravens some sparklies, and Maya explained that we're all very nice and their boss is a jerk.

OT: That stopped them?

EF: Definitely. Ravens are way smart. I think they might unionize. Anyway, when the raven idea didn't work, he started mumbling something and this weird black smoke started gathering around him. Chiara was awake by now, and she just shoved a gag in his mouth. Then he sort of, um, passed out again.

OT: He passed out?

EF: The smell was pretty intense.

OT: ...

EF: [whispering] Wyvern scat.

OT: Got it.

EF: We were worried he would wake up and do something else, so next she stuck him in her mirror. It was really nice of her to sacrifice it—she loved that mirror.

OT: It's going to be hard to get him out for his trial.

EF: [shrugging]

Secret Sister note from [redacted] to Eliza F.

> Eliza! You are literally the very best person on the whole planet. You saved all of us, and I will never forget that. Thank you so much. I wish I could have seen you smack that prince with the Dutch oven. I bet it was amazing. I think maybe I want to take up baseball now too. Never know when you're going to need to smack some evil villain upside the head, right?
>
> But seriously, thank you, Eliza. We all owe you big time.
>
> Sincerely,
>
> Your Secret Sister

Note from Eliza F. to Sister Beth Larsen, slipped inside her scripture bag

Hi, Sister Larsen. Thank you for putting together such a great camp. I know it kind of ended badly, but I just wanted to say thanks. I wasn't sure I was going to come this year. Anyway, I'm so glad I came. I mean, for the obvious reasons of course, but also because it was nice to feel needed and seen (except by evil princes, thankfully). Thanks again for everything,
Eliza

Email from Sister Beth Larsen to Sister Andrea Druce, ward historian, 30 January 2026

Re: Young Women group contribution to the Forest Thicket 2nd Ward 2025 History

Hi, Sister Druce. Thanks for reaching out. Sorry it took me so long to get back to you. It's been hard thinking about how to encapsulate such an interesting year. Here you go, hope it helps!
Sister Larsen

The Young Women have had an eventful year. They have learned a variety of practical and beautifying skills, including various fiber arts, cobbler making, and budget balancing. They have started a baseball club, inviting young women from other local wards to join in. They have also begun attending a weekly martial arts/self-defense class together.

Camp was especially noteworthy, as the Young Women were attacked by the infamous Prince Tignan of the Dark Forest, who was masquerading as a friendly local prince. Thanks to the team efforts of our impressive Young Women, the prince was defeated and is now awaiting trial.

As a side note, it turns out that Prince Tignan was the source of the dark presence people used to talk about in the forest, so I guess parents will have to start a new rumor to keep little kids from wandering into the woods. [Sister Druce: You can delete that line if you want. People might not get that I'm kidding.]

Through all of the challenges and adventures of this year, the Young Women really learned that, as Elder Eyring said, when you are doing God's work, "you will be magnified, and you do not work alone."

Additionally, after much discussion and prayer, the Young Women have decided that, though it has been a hundred-year tradition to hold camp on the edge of the Dark Forest, next year we will be glamping at a hot springs spa and resort.

Wolfskin

Once upon a time, there was a young tradesman who lived in the foothills, a foolish man who believed he should be given all he wanted, no matter the cost to others. One night in the tavern, when ale had loosened the tongues of the men, he heard the story of a beautiful young woman who lived in the mountains. In the daylight, it was said, she lived as a wolf in the forest. But when she wanted to, she could shed her wolfskin and become human, the most gorgeous woman imaginable—lithe and lovely, russet hair swirling around her the same shade as the wolf's fur, with golden eyes like the beast.

The stories went on as the ale flowed. "I saw her once, staring at me, as close to me as you are," declared one man.

"She came to me as a wolf," said another. "Knocked me down and stood over me like she wanted to chew me up."

"Then how come you're not dead?" someone asked, and at the speaker's stuttered reply, drunken laughter swept through the room. The young man listened quietly as an idea began to form in his mind.

He would find the woman and take her to wife.

So he began to lay his trap. He'd heard that the woman was curious, drawn by light and the unknown. He built up a bonfire and laid out foods that would be unfamiliar and strange to one who had lived in the forest. Then he stood in the shadows and waited.

Soon enough she came: a great red wolf with eyes a shade too human. She paced back and forth, outside the edge of the fire's light, tempted but wary. The scent of the food covered the scent of the man. Finally, when it seemed she would draw away, she glanced around in a furtive manner that was certainly not the way of a beast. Then she dropped her wolfskin and walked forward.

The man sucked in his breath as the firelight fell on her. A wolf's ears would have caught the sound, but she was all human now. She moved with the grace of a wild animal, but she was drawn to the fire as the wild would never be.

Faster than flame, he ran to where she had discarded her skin. He snatched it up and fled to hide it. When finally she had exhausted her curiosity, she found that her wolfskin was gone.

She howled in grief and fear, the human in her too weak to think of what to do. Here was the first secret of the wolfwoman: She was bound to her wolfskin, and to lose that connection caused her anguish.

And thus, when she learned who held that skin, she was bound to him as well. At first she thought of finding it, stealing it back from him—but he had hidden it too cleverly. In time, when she realized what he wanted from her, she determined that she would give it so that she could stay close to her wolfskin. One day he would make a mistake. One day she would find that wolfskin, and on that day she would take it up and strike, her claws tearing into flesh, giving way to the satisfying crunch of broken bone beneath her jaw.

But she would have to bide her time.

So, in the way of humans, she was bound to him in marriage.

In time the man, who had thought only to possess her, began to see that she was not only beautiful but also kind. The children of the village would flock to her, following her around both for her beauty and for her strangeness. There is nothing that appeals to a child so much as mystery. And when they came to her, she would stop in her task and play with them or sing. She never spoke, only sang sweet, wordless tunes. Her voice was mournful and sharp, like the howl of the wolf on the mountain. The children hovered near her.

But the man could see her kindness only from a distance, for she did not share it with him. With him she was a caged beast, watching and waiting, refusing to be tamed. He began to see what he had not seen before—that he could not force such beauty to be his. But still he feared to let it go. If he could not have it, he at least wished to be near it. So he kept her wolfskin hidden from her, and he kept her bound.

Now, I mentioned that when the children came, she would stop in her tasks. There was one task that she favored above all others—that of knitting. Herein lies the second great secret of the wolfwoman. She was bound, it is true, to the man who had taken her hide. But there was a way to win free, as there always is in such tales.

It would take seven years, and during that time she could not speak, but if she spent the time knitting herself a new wolfskin, she could be free again. One word, and she would lose her chance.

Though the man did not release her, he did all else that he could to treat her kindly. He brought her gifts of clothing and food she liked, making sure she had time to play with the village children as she loved to do. In giving, he began to learn the meaning of love.

So the years passed, and she knitted, and he watched.

But as the fifth year came, he finally realized it and admitted it to himself—he would never have her willingly. So he went to the place where he had hidden her skin years before. He brought it to her and placed it at her feet, drawing back to watch what she would do.

Half expecting to be dead any minute, claws sunk deep into his chest.

The wolfwoman looked away from her knitting, down to where her skin and her freedom lay before her. She looked up at him wordlessly, searching his face.

"I'm sorry" is all he said before he could not bear to look at her again. He turned away, waiting for her to take her skin and go. She drew it up into her lap, rubbing its softness against her human cheek, but she did not put it on. She breathed it in, the wild scent of the forest still clinging to the wolfskin after all this time.

Then she folded it gently and set it beside her.

She picked up her needles and continued to knit. When another two years had come and gone, she took the finished wolfskin and gave it to her husband. They both pulled on their skins and went out into the mountains to howl and run together, then they returned to the village. They lived both lives, the wild and the tame, and did so happily ever after.

Siren's Younger Sister

KALINA SIGHED AS ANOTHER ship approached the island. A little closer, and her sister would start singing. She gathered a few dozen earplugs and boarded her rescue boat.

The haunting music began drifting over the waves, and the ship staggered in the water. It veered suddenly, rushing toward the rocks surrounding the island. Kalina was already navigating her own boat through the treacherous waters toward it. By the time she got to the floundering ship, it had crashed, and passengers were thrashing in the waves.

Ligeia stopped singing. She usually only cared about the performance, rarely watching the aftermath. Kalina threw out her life preservers and dragged the survivors onto her boat, giving them earplugs anyway, just in case.

She heaved a dark-haired man onto the deck and checked his pulse. His heartbeat was steady, and he didn't seem injured, so she'd almost moved on to the next victim when he opened his eyes. They were a lovely deep green. He blinked at her silhouette, backlit by the afternoon sun. "Mermaids?" he asked feebly, then fell unconscious.

Kalina rolled her eyes. Humans were so predictable.

Hours later, Kalina had settled everyone into neat rows of cots and attended to the injured. The green-eyed man still slept, and she inspected him more closely. She'd seen her share of handsome men, but she didn't mind seeing another.

As if he felt her eyes, he woke, looked straight at her, and groaned. "Ergh, what happened?" He rubbed his forehead. "Did I call you a mermaid?"

"It's a pretty common reaction."

"I blame my sisters. We watched a lot of Disney."

Not the worst thing you could blame a sister for, she thought. "My name isn't Ariel."

He chuckled. "So what is it?"

"Kalina," she said.

"Aaron."

"Nice to meet you."

"Thanks for saving me." He groaned again, and Kalina reached for a bottle of painkillers. "So what *did* happen? I just remember music... and then chaos."

Kalina liked this one, so she decided to tell him the truth. "You fell victim to my sister, Ligeia. She's a siren—like from mythology. She sings, you crash, I rescue. It's kind of our thing."

Aaron stared. "You're kidding," he finally said.

"Nope."

"That's... unexpected." He winced again. "Pretty close to mermaids, though."

The next few days were far nicer than she was used to after a shipwreck. Aaron chatted with her as she helped the others, and he recovered quickly, and then he began helping too. It was pleasant, and he was funny, and she found herself, against her better judgment, falling in love.

"You ever think about leaving the island?" Aaron asked.

Kalina grimaced. "I'm bound here with Ligeia. Neither of us can leave. I can barely get past the rocks to save the shipwrecks. Trust me, I've tried. But it's not so bad. I have a magical ship to send back our victims; I've got a fulfilling career helping others; I've got beach hair women would kill for."

He laughed, a sound Kalina was growing to love. "How do you know so much about the rest of the world?"

"Google, of course."

"You have internet?"

"Doesn't everybody?"

"It gets through your magical barrier?"

"It's tricky, and I've had to work a lot of tech mumbo jumbo with some washed-up electronics, but yeah, I can get a signal." She shook her head in despair. "Not enough to stream *The Mandalorian*, though."

"Tragedy."

Bit by bit, Kalina and Aaron learned about each other's lives. Kalina's sister was a prima donna who loved having an audience, even if it killed them. Aaron was a director doing small-time work for a big

TV company. He finally brought up the subject they'd both avoided. "I have to leave eventually," he said.

She frowned. "I know."

"But I'd like to come back."

Her eyes darted to his in hope until she remembered. "You can't. Once you pass the magical barrier around our island, you forget everything." She took a breath. "You'll forget about me."

An idea came to her a few days later as he explained the recording equipment he'd brought on the ship, parts of which had washed ashore. It probably wouldn't work, but it was the best chance they had. She stewed over it another day as she repaired his recording equipment. It was crucial to the plan.

"Will it work?" he asked.

"Honestly? I don't know. But it's all I can think of." She looked away, uncertain. "It requires a lot from you. You'll have to do all the convincing. And the remembering."

He smiled reassuringly. "I will *not* forget you. As for the convincing? That's my job."

She smiled too, hiding her sadness and fear. According to the plan, he'd be leaving in a few days, maybe forever.

Two months later she woke to an unexpected but hoped-for sound. A ship, sailing carefully through the rocks, even though Ligeia was singing. Could it be?

She ran to the shore to find workers with earplugs already unloading huge boxes. She scanned the faces for one in particular.

"You came back," she yelled.

He removed his earplugs and met her halfway across the sand. "Of course."

"The recording worked!" They'd spent several days recording endless details of the island to help him remember it once he'd left.

"The pitch worked too. Your island is now a destination for next season's *Reality Shipwreck Island*." His gaze warmed her skin. "The contracts will be ridiculously complicated, and the broadcast will be tough, but I told them I knew someone who could work the tech." He winked.

She smiled. It sounded amazing, and she thought even Ligeia would love it. Millions of listeners every week. Good thing recording canceled out her voice's power.

"And guess who's going to direct?" He pointed to himself. "Looks like I'll be sticking around."

Her smile widened, and she put her arms around his neck. "That's music to my ears."

Spun from Linen and Lies

AUTHOR'S NOTE:

This story is a sequel to "Forged in Iron and Blood" and contains spoilers. Please read "Forged in Iron and Blood" first.

"Do you think he's still following us?" Seelah turned on the cart's bench to scan the dusty road behind them.

Lina glanced into the sky instead. There was nothing on the road for miles, but somewhere above, a morhawk was no doubt circling, waiting to report to its master. "Yes," she said with certainty.

They'd noticed him in the shadows one day, a lithe, enigmatic figure who bore the traces of long-held authority: a confident stride, movements that said he cared little what others thought of him. A truthseer.

"At least it's not those other fellows," Seelah said with her customary cheer.

And she was right. Far better a truthseer, one who was committed to justice for human and fae alike, than Tyblith and his cursed torque.

Lina nodded, and the cart rolled its way into town. Dryss was small, but the rows of houses and shops were neat. The manor house sat on a hill overlooking the other buildings, and everything was orderly, just so. It should have felt charming and friendly.

Somehow, though, despite the order, the place looked exhausted. It was in the faded paint of the shutters, the weeds popping up amid flowers, and most of all in the quiet of the people. No small children ran laughing through the streets. The few people out on errands seemed tired and withdrawn.

No one approached the newcomers. No curious looks followed them. "Not an auspicious beginning."

"No, but someone here will be happy to see us." Seelah glanced meaningfully at the unconscious man in the back of the cart.

"Let's hope so."

"Hello," Seelah called to an older woman bustling past. "We found a man from your village. He's—"

"Is he dead then?" the woman interrupted. She shook her head. "I knew it."

"No," Seelah rushed on. "Not dead, but injured. He needs care. Do you know who he is and where to find his family?" Seelah waved the woman forward to look into the cart and identify him.

She didn't bother. "That'll be Seftin." She pointed down the road. "You'll find his place down that way, at the mill. His daughter should be there. Tell her we're sorry." She shook her head and turned away to enter a shop.

Lina looked after her. "Did that seem strange to you?"

Seelah nodded. "She expected him to be dead."

Lina clucked to the horses and sat in silence as they plodded on.

Seelah rolled her eyes. "I can almost hear you thinking."

"It's odd, that's all."

"And before you know it, we'll be embroiled in someone else's troubles again."

"It hasn't happened that many times."

"Only almost every place we've been since we left," Seelah chided. But there was a smile in her voice.

"You could go back home, you know."

"Don't even suggest it. I'm having more fun traveling and getting into trouble with you than I've had since my dear Himleh died."

"Well then," Lina said, pointing to the mill they could see now at the edge of town, "looks like it's time to get into a bit more."

The mill was sturdy and strong, with a fair-sized house attached to it, and a stream running behind them both. Lina felt the familiar itch of discomfort that always accompanied running water. The stream was calm though, and only strong enough for a small millstone, so she could manage being near it.

"Halloo," she called. "We need your help."

A young woman, maybe in her early twenties, appeared at the door. She wiped her hands on the apron at her waist and looked at Lina and Seelah with a wary expression. "Yes?" she asked.

"We have a man in our cart. We were told he might be your father?"

The young woman's face blanched and she ran forward. "Papi?"

"He's been injured," Seelah added quickly. "But I think he's going to be fine, just needs rest."

The woman had already climbed into the back of the cart and was stroking her father's hair back. "Papi? Are you all right? I'm sorry we sent you. We should have known it wouldn't work." She bent and kissed his forehead. "I'm sorry."

Lina and Seelah exchanged a glanced. What wouldn't work?

Seelah bustled around to the young woman's side. "Why don't we help you get him inside?"

Lina clambered down from the cart and set aside the walking stick she'd taken to using. She could do without it for a bit. With a bit of maneuvering, the three of them managed to get him into the house. Once they'd settled him into his bed, the woman ushered them out of his room, through a small parlor, and into a broad kitchen, where she gestured for them to sit.

"Thank you for bringing him back to me," she said, her voice resigned. "What can I do to repay you?"

They looked at each other.

"I can't pay you any money," she added quickly, her expression worried.

Seelah shook her head. "No, no, dear. We wouldn't dream of taking money. Any decent person would have done it. No, we were just thinking it's been a long day. I'm sure there's an inn somewhere in town, but we're bone tired. Do you have space we could stay here for the night? Just a couple pallets in the corner of a room would be enough, if you could manage it."

The young woman's expression cleared. "Oh, that I can manage, along with a bite to eat. Nothing fancy, but some warm soup, if that sounds good."

Lina smiled broadly. "It sounds delicious. But first, perhaps introductions are in order. I'm Lina." She gestured to Seelah. "And this is my friend Seelah. We were traveling up north when we found your father on the road."

He'd been beaten severely, and they'd thought him dead at first. Anything he'd carried was gone aside from the clothes on his back—clothing of a finer weave than Lina would have expected on a commoner, but in a style made for work rather than fashion. They'd spent the last two days nursing him carefully and bringing him back to Dryss.

"I'm Dedru, and my father is Seftin. Thank you again for bringing him back."

"Of course," Seelah said. "And if you have a bit of spare flour from your mill, how about I make something to go with the soup."

"Flour we have, but not much more, I'm afraid." Dedru gave a tired smiled as she showed Seelah around the kitchen. For its size, the supplies and pantry were surprisingly sparse, the shelves and cabinets far too bare.

"Just the flour is good enough. I'll come up with something." Seelah bustled Dedru out of the kitchen. "You go take care of your father, and I'll let you know when the food is ready."

Seelah could turn almost anything into a delicious meal, so much so that Lina sometimes joked she must have a drop of fae blood. The real fae powers were specific and named, but you often found someone with a whiff of otherwise-unspecified magic as well. It was the kind of thing that showed up as never burning the bread or a mesmerizing singing voice or, perhaps, irresistible pastries.

While Seelah cooked, Lina went with Dedru to tend to the injured man. He needed a change of clothing and a rinse for his hot forehead. As they were finishing up, Seelah arrived with a small cup of broth, which Dedru dribbled into his mouth for a few minutes before they finally tucked him into bed.

Back in the kitchen, they sat in silence and ate the soup and bread, and Lina noticed that Dedru seemed to relax a bit under the influence of warm, fresh biscuits.

"Thank you again," she finally said. "I don't know what would have happened if you hadn't helped him."

"No use thinking about that, dear." Seelah patted Dedru's arm. "Your father's going to be fine soon enough. Think of that instead."

Lina rose and gathered her dishes to wash. "Please, let us know if you need something during the night."

Dedru nodded, but her thoughts seemed to be elsewhere. She showed them down the hallway to a small room with two beds. The mildew of disuse hung in the air, but Dedru opened the window for a soft breeze. Lina wondered who the beds had once belonged to, but the downcast look on Dedru's face told her not to ask.

A few minutes of fluffing pillows and pulling out soft, worn quilts, and Seelah and Lina were left alone. They settled into their beds, and

Lina sighed. Something was wrong here, but at least she could have one night of sleep on a lovely soft surface, under the comfort of a thick blanket, before she had to consider what.

Tozo watched as Vestus flew slow, lazy circles on the updrafts above him. Eventually the morhawk would come down, once he saw where the women were going next, and then Tozo would keep following. It was a leisurely way to hunt, but Tozo wasn't in a hurry. This was a perk of his job. When he wasn't on official business, he had the freedom to decide how to spend his time, what crimes to pursue. In fact, he was expected to wander like this, always keeping an eye out for potential trouble.

And those two women were definitely potential trouble.

He'd noticed them first a few towns back, with that business of the thieving neighbors. They were intriguing, unexpected, hiding things. Even though he'd not seen anything illegal by either human or fae code—had even heard several positive reports of their actions—he couldn't let them go. Not quite yet.

Maybe he would give up on them after this next town or two, but he could afford to be patient awhile yet. He'd not had any messages brought by any of the other truthseers' morhawks, so he had nothing more urgent to do. He rode on, still wondering what the women were up to.

He suspected they'd caught him following them in the last town, maybe even before. He didn't think he'd gotten sloppy, so it came as a surprise when their movements suddenly became more careful. Apparently he needed to be more careful too.

A cry from above drew his attention. Vestus was back. With a dive and a swoop, the magnificent bird landed on his shoulder. Tozo smiled and pulled out a small chunk of rabbit as a treat.

Tozo stroked the bird and waited as he ate. In a moment, the treat was gone, and Vestus signaled which direction they should take.

South and west. No great surprise there, since the road hadn't branched throughout the day, but it was good to know he hadn't been led astray. He checked his map. He was headed for Dryss. The last little town on the edges of the kingdom.

He could ride another couple of hours, make it to town, and sleep in a real bed this night, or he could stay outside. The only advantage to staying outside town was to avoid the women. But if they already knew he was following, that didn't matter. His appearance so near them might even rattle them into making foolish errors he could catch.

Plus, a real meal would be welcome. The thought of stew over a hearth, or perhaps a bit of soft bread, decided him. He would ride into town. No sense hiding anymore.

Lina opened her eyes to stare up at the dark ceiling. Some sound had awakened her, and adrenaline flowed through her veins as she prepared, yet again, for danger.

It would be nice to not be preparing for danger.

She waited and listened, her hand sliding slowly to where she'd hid a small dagger in her bed.

Another moment and she heard the sound again. A murmur of voices, coming from down the hall. She sat up and glanced over at Seelah's bed. She, too, was awake.

Lina put her finger to her lips and rose.

She'd checked the floor the night before for creaks, so she knew how to move quietly across the room. She crept to the door and opened it. The murmur of voices became louder, but still not loud enough to hear the words.

She could leave it alone. She could go back to her bed, back to sleep, back to the nightmares that still sometimes came.

But there was a timbre to the voices that spoke worry.

The hallway down to the kitchen and parlor turned, so Lina was safe from discovery as long as she was very quiet. She looked back at Seelah, who nodded. She would not be able to make this journey as quietly as Lina, so she'd wait until Lina returned with a report.

Lina sidled down the hallway. Pale flickers of candlelight led her way toward the parlor.

"—we knew it was a dim hope," one female voice whispered.

"We shouldn't have sent him," another said.

"What choice did we have?" a third voice asked.

"It doesn't matter," said a fourth voice that sounded like Dedru, though it was hard to tell when all the voices were whispered. "What matters is what happens next."

"Your own father, and you say it doesn't matter?" one asked, incredulous.

Dedru sighed. "I don't mean it. I just... I can't afford to think about it. He's alive, and that's better than we might have expected. Please"—her voice broke—"let me work on the problem instead of worrying."

There was a murmur of sympathy.

"So what do we do next?"

"I've run out of ideas. You?"

None of the other voices responded for a moment.

"Do you think we could use the travelers?" someone asked.

"Doubtful," Dedru dismissed. "They're just two old women passing through. They won't have any better connections than we do."

"But we might be able to sneak a message out with them."

"And put them in danger as well? Without warning them?" The voice rose in anger. "We will not stoop to that."

Dedru shushed her. "Careful. But you're right, we all know the risks. They don't."

Folk were in trouble. Folk were always in trouble, somewhere. But in this case, folk were in trouble right in front of her. It wasn't the sort of thing Lina had ever been good at ignoring. She'd kept herself in check in Solime, hiding there as she was. But she wasn't hiding the same way anymore. She didn't have to ignore it when people were in need.

She glanced back toward her room apologetically. Poor Seelah, getting sucked into trouble again. Then again, she did say she enjoyed the adventure.

Lina stepped into the room and into the candlelight. "Then why don't you tell us?"

Dedru gasped and rose from her chair. Three other young women stared at her from around the room, pale with fear.

"Lina-wanderer. I'm so sorry, I didn't hear you awaken. We were just..." Dedru trailed off and looked to the other women for help.

"Just discussing poor Dedru's father," one of them said smoothly. "Deciding how best to care for him."

"Yes." Dedru nodded. Impressive, the speed with which she regained her composure—the speed with which they all regained composure, actually. They almost looked as if they were simply discussing the weather. "But I'm so sorry we woke you."

Lina shook her head. "No, it will be much simpler if we don't pretend. You are in some sort of trouble. You have been for quite some time, and you're running out of ideas."

The women still fought valiantly to look nonchalant, but Lina could tell they were struck by how much she'd overheard.

"You need some help, apparently, but we're just two old women, and we won't be much help. That's where you're wrong, though." She looked back toward the hallway. "Seelah?" she called.

Seelah appeared mere seconds later. She'd clearly been ready to jump into the fray. Lina smiled.

"Yes? Something for us to do?" Seelah asked, taking in the women grouped around the parlor with a glance. "Oh dear. Not a young man, I hope?"

Lina laughed. "I doubt a foolish young man is their problem. They look clever enough to have solved a problem of romance without much fuss."

A thin brunette looked mollified, but the others remained tense and suspicious.

Lina turned serious. "We're more help in a tight spot than you might imagine," she said gently. "You might try us."

One of the women—this one with thick black hair and an upturned nose—asked suspiciously, "Why would you want to help us? And how do we know we can trust you?"

Lina and Seelah looked at each other. How much could they reveal?

"We like to be helpful, when we can," Lina said with a shrug. It was a true, if somewhat simplified, explanation.

"As to trust... That's difficult, isn't it? You'll have to decide for yourselves after we've talked." She looked around at the women, and Lina knew exactly what she would say next. "But first, food. How you can discuss dire situations without a bite to eat is beyond me."

Someone gave a snort of laughter. Lina was inclined to agree.

Seelah swept out of the parlor and into the kitchen. She'd be rifling through the basket she'd left there—the smaller one, filled with Seelah's favorite seasonings. Pleasant aromas would be wafting from the kitchen in no time.

Lina sat down. "Let me tell you about us." She hesitated. "There is... much I cannot tell, but I'll say what I can." And she spent the next several minutes laying out the loose details of some of their past months of travel and the little ways they'd been able to help those they'd come across.

The women listened, saying nothing. The tension in the room was palpable, and Lina had no idea if she was getting through to them. In the end, she simply stopped explaining and said, "You have no way of knowing if we tell the truth. We can only offer assurances, and you will have to decide what you want to do with them."

Seelah came into the room then with some quick griddle cakes, and she set a plate of them on a small table. "Eat while you decide." When the young women looked suspiciously at the food, Seelah took the top pastry and began to nibble at it happily.

Lina took a pastry from the middle of the pile and ate as well. After a moment, the others began to pass the plate around and eat.

"If you'd like, we can remove ourselves while you discuss your decision," Lina added after a minute or two of silent chewing.

The young women looked at one another around the table, silent conversation flying between them.

After another moment, Dedru gave one short decisive nod. "We will tell you, though I doubt you can do anything for us."

Lina and Seelah said nothing.

Dedru made short work of introducing the young women. The brunette was Jhissa. Mevi was the suspicious black-haired girl. The fourth, younger and quieter than the others, was Vira.

Lina nodded to each, then turned back to Dedru—clearly the leader—to hear their story.

She squared her shoulders and began. "Dryss is small, as you see, and off by itself. We rely on our lord to help when things get hard, and in return we have always served him. We've done well."

Lina thought of the thin, wary faces of the townspeople they'd passed on their way through town. There must be a "but" coming.

"Two years ago, marauders came. We weren't ready. We've always been safe here. They struck too fast for us to send for help." Dedru closed her eyes briefly. The air was heavy with sadness.

Mevi took up the story. "Many of our people fought. Many of them died. Lord Dorin led them. And he died with them."

"Dorin was a good lord," Vira added in a quiet voice. "We are mostly a textile village, both linen and wool. We do all the tending, harvesting, spinning, and weaving ourselves." That explained the soft texture of Seftin's clothing. "Lord Dorin always arranged for our goods to be taken away and traded for all our other needs. His taxes were fair. We were doing well."

Dedru took up the story again. "His son survived the raids and became our new lord. Corym." She said the name with distaste. "He'd always been a climber—off at parties with higher-ups, trying to impress them. But we figured when he took on the lordship he'd settle in a bit. He said he would take care of us, and we believed him."

"We were stupid," Mevi declared.

"Yes," Dedru agreed. "We were. But we didn't see what was happening. He hired a new trader, a fae fellow we'd seen with him before. Comes through about once a month. Takes away all our goods. Comes back with a pittance that's getting smaller every time."

"Last winter made it worse. More of the townspeople died off than usual, and more of the sheep. There's always a few—old ones, or sickly—but it was a bad year. Fewer skilled people to do the work, less wool to spin, but still all the growing children to feed." The women took up the story from each other easily, a seamless flow of words from one to the other.

"The weather wasn't his fault, but he kept expecting the same wares from us, giving us less and less in exchange."

"So we started trying to work around him. Sent our cloth to market with one of our men instead of Corym's trader—but no one would deal with us, or the wares got damaged along the way, or they got stolen."

The robberies were unusual, just like the marauders had been. This area was one of the safest in the kingdom.

"That's what my father was doing when you found him," Dedru said. "He'd taken some of our best cloth to sell."

"We sent messages to the magistrates. We even wrote to the king, asking him to help us."

"The letters disappeared, or we never got a response. The only time someone answered was an official message saying they'd heard nothing but good reports of Corym, and we must be lying. No offer to check up on him, no offers of aid."

Strange. The king was known for fairness and justice. "Who took the letters?" Lina asked. Maybe they'd been bribed not to deliver them.

Mevi answered the unspoken question. "We thought about that already. Wondering if the messengers could be trusted. Sent them with townspeople too, people we knew we could trust."

"And there's always something. Letter goes astray, messenger gets hurt. A magistrate came to town once but refused to even ask Lord Corym questions, no matter what we tried to explain about him and the trader. It all sounds like we're just complaining or making things up."

They weren't wrong. On the surface it did sound like simply a heap of bad luck, a terrible lord, and a lot of complaining. Nothing all that unusual—and nothing that couldn't be cleared up with a bit of aid to the town and an investigation into the lord's behaviors. The fact that no aid had been given, no investigation made… That was the troublesome part.

"Why don't you move away? Pack up and go?" Lina asked.

"Some have, a few who were free enough. We don't hear from them anymore. For the rest of us, it's not that easy, is it?"

It wasn't. Even if Lina had done it several times now.

"And he has the children."

"What?"

"The children of the village. Last year, after the sickness, he offered to set up a little 'school' for the young ones who'd been orphaned or only had one parent left after the raids and sickness."

"He brought them to live in the castle, feed them, keep them safe."

"It seemed so kind."

"He said they'd learn to read and write, but mostly they're learning how to be servants in his manor."

Mevi snorted. "Without being paid."

"Half the children live in his manor half the year. Then he switches. He always has half of them."

"Someone tried last year to flirt with him, get close enough to give him something to… stop him permanently," Jhissa said quietly.

No one would meet Lina's or Seelah's eyes.

Dedru went on hastily. "She got sick instead, almost killed her. But somehow he was fine."

"It wasn't given to the wrong person by mistake?"

Mevi shook her head. "Definitely not. It didn't affect him at all, like it slid right off him into me." She clearly didn't care if Lina and Seelah knew she was an attempted assassin.

"Strange," Lina murmured.

"There's just… something," Dedru said, defeated. "We can't figure it. Everything he does seems to turn to his good. Even the winter that hurt the rest of us—he just sailed through, got a reputation for helping the nearby towns. Meanwhile here we were dying."

The room fell silent for a moment with memories of the past.

Seelah finally broke the silence. "And why is it left to the four of you to solve this problem?"

Dedru shrugged. "There used to be more of us, but most of them have given up or been beaten down by it all. Or they're getting older or just too afraid."

Lina thought of the woman they'd met in the village, so certain Seftin was dead.

"Tell us more about your lord. His trader, his friends, anything else you can think of." Seelah passed another plate of griddle cakes around.

So they did. Lord Corym sounded like an unremarkable man. Had never been much trouble before his father died—but also hadn't been much use. Often away from town, making friends with higher ranks, trying to insinuate himself into their society. He'd always looked down on the townspeople, but not much more than was common with the nobility.

He didn't appear to drink, gamble, or chase women overmuch. His primary vice was an obvious, voracious desire to be seen as more important than he was, to rise in society. His noble friends were nothing out of the ordinary, and the fae trader who came through town every month was charismatic and flirtatious, but never going too far in his attentions, and absolutely closed-mouthed when it came to business.

"That's all I can think of," Dedru finally concluded. The hour had worn later, and everyone drooped with the weight of sleeplessness and the situation.

Lina nodded sharply and stood. "We will think on it and see what we can do." Nothing was clear yet. She and Seelah would have to observe the lordling and the town for themselves. See if they could catch something the townspeople had not.

"Thank you," Dedru said, and the others murmured agreement, but there was little hope behind the words as they rose and prepared to depart. Lina couldn't blame them.

"Do take some cakes with you as you leave," Seelah said with a smile, and she pushed one last warm pastry into each woman's hand.

It took over a week. They spent the time wandering through the shops and neighborhoods, meeting townspeople, asking casual questions, with Lina leaning on her walking stick and Seelah carrying her basket. Two old ladies innocently traveling the world. Little new information came from their search though—the young women had been quite thorough.

They'd seen the truthseer around town as well, haunting them silently as before. Never approaching, never menacing, just... there. Something would have to be done about him, but what? He couldn't arrest them, as they'd never done anything illegal. But truthseers could sense fae magic—both its presence in an object and the *use* of that magic, and it worried them to know he was watching.

If Lina made a mistake, if someone made an idle promise to her while he was near, he would see the truth of what she was. Oathbinding itself wasn't a crime, but it would make her infinitely more interesting and put them both in danger.

So they stayed as far from him as they could, while always knowing he was near, and they sought for the source of the town's problems.

"What do you think of this yarn?" Seelah asked as they walked along. She pulled a length of soft green wool from her basket. "I thought I'd knit a scarf for Mohn."

"I'm sure he'll love it," Lina said absently, watching the faces of those they passed. Would they ever discover the source of the problem?

Seelah nudged Lina's shoulder. "I know you're barely paying attention, Lina."

"Sorry. Just thinking."

"It's fine. Oh look, there's Mevi." Seelah pointed across the road to where Mevi walked with a stack of pots in her arms. "I'll ask her."

Before she could cross, a shout came from behind. "Make way!"

They shuffled to the side as a tall young man rode down the street with two servants on horses behind him.

Lina eyed the man. This was the lordling, finally. They hadn't been able to see him in person until now. He didn't come out among the rabble much.

He rode proudly—his chin up, his eyes skimming over the townspeople on the road as if they didn't exist. He had fine dark hair, a good jawline, and dark eyes. A handsome man, if you didn't count his obvious arrogance. His clothing was impeccable—dark blue and green linen, finely embroidered, likely the best that Dryss had to offer.

"Well, isn't he a fancy piece of work?" Seelah muttered.

Lina nodded but didn't take her eyes off him. There was something odd, something... She squinted. A pendant?

Her eyes skimmed his clothing. Impeccable embroidery. The townspeople must have provided their best. But what was around his neck? Something unusual. She leaned forward to look closer.

His clothing was well-tailored from a fine linen. Dryss did indeed make beautiful fabrics. Other ornamentation was sparse, but... something lay on a chain around his neck.

She looked away from it, immediately registering his fine clothing again. She blinked and shook her head. Something was wrong. Every time she tried to look at that pendant, her thoughts slid elsewhere.

It made her all the more determined to pay attention. Thoughts of mindturning entered her head. *Please don't let it be that.*

She blinked again, this time focusing all her concentration. The piece was small, almost shockingly modest for the rest of his outfit. It—

A flash of movement came from across the street, along with a loud series of clattering bangs as a collection of pots and pans rolled into the road.

The lordling's horse reared at the sound and the metal pots' reflections in the sunlight. The servants' horses shied out of its way. Corym fought for control of his horse, but it continued to rear back as the pots and pans kept clattering across its way.

Another second, and Corym lost control entirely. One moment he was on his horse's back, and the next he was flying off it... directly into the path of another horse's hooves.

Lina flinched in expectation of the crunch of bones, but none came. Somehow—even watching him carefully, she couldn't quite see how—he rolled out of the way, avoiding every single hoof crashing to the ground. Several potential killing blows, and they all... just didn't strike.

Seelah sucked in a breath beside her. "Blood of a nix," she muttered.

Lina nodded. The luck on this man was incredible.

The luck.

Could it be as simple as that? No, surely not. And yet... she hadn't been able to really look at his pendant.

Lord Corym was standing now, dusting off his jacket and yelling. Mevi had somehow disappeared down the street, so he had no one to rail at other than his servants. The haste of Mevi's flight suggested this had been no accident. Yet once again, Lord Corym escaped all injury.

Lina watched him, ignoring his anger, waiting for him to turn toward her. When he did, she sucked in a breath. The pendant he'd worn was easier to see now—no longer a bright gold, now dulled to a brownish bronze. This was not mindturning, no, and not as terrible. Still, the clues fell into place. The way fortune seemed to favor this man, the way the townspeople seemed to diminish. Not mindturning, but something almost as illegal and taboo.

A small crowd had formed, with Vira among them, looking anxious and disappointed.

Lina approached her. "I must meet with all of you," she whispered urgently. "Gather the others and come to the mill as soon as you can."

Vira gave one small nod and scurried to spread the news, while Lina's head whirled.

It took less than an hour to gather them. Lina looked into the faces of the young women assembled, almost as she had seen them that first night. So young but so brave, so willing to do whatever it took to protect what remained of their home and their people. Seftin was getting better but still sleeping much of the time; he was in bed right now, so they kept their voices quiet.

"Your lordling is working with a luckspinner," she said without preamble.

The young women's expressions remained blank.

"A luckspinner is a member of the fae—probably the trader, based on what you've told us—who takes physical goods and 'spins' them into a talisman that stores luck."

"Stores luck?"

Lina nodded. "Making the talisman owner unnaturally fortunate. Based on what you've told me, I imagine most of his luck is being used to curry favor with higher aristocracy and nobles—that's his primary goal. But I suspect he's also using it in a more general sense to keep his secrets safe."

"And of course to keep *himself* safe," Seelah added, with a pointed glance at Mevi.

The women murmured among themselves, digesting this news.

"If luckspinning exists," Dedru asked, "why doesn't everyone do it? Any fae who can use it should be doing it all the time."

Lina shook her head. The fae were very secretive about their various gifts. At times she was grateful—her whole existence depended on secrecy. But times like this, she wished all humans knew the rules of the fae. "No. The fae have strict rules. A luckspinner is never to spin only for himself. He is allowed to take the tiniest portion of the luck he spins, but most of it must go to the one he spins for. That's the first rule. The second is that the receiver of the luck must be the one to create the physical goods being used." She paused.

"But what does Lord Corym create?" Jhissa asked.

Mevi saw it immediately. "He doesn't. He's been using *our* goods to get *his* luck."

Lina nodded. "Yes. It's a breach of fae law, but it's also challenging to prove. Luckspinning is slippery, which is likely why no one has recognized it. Have you happened to notice the jewelry he wears?"

Dedru furrowed her brow. "No. You?" She turned to the others. All of them shook their heads. "Why does that matter?"

"The one who receives the luck must wear the talisman, and it tarnishes when used. But they resist being noticed or found out."

"Then how did *you* notice it?" Mevi asked suspiciously.

"I pay attention to jewelry. The more it doesn't want to be seen, the more I pay attention." Lina hoped her stiff tone left no room for questions.

Mevi eyed Lina for a moment. Whatever she saw seemed to satisfy her. She gave a quick nod.

"But what about the cloth?" Jhissa asked. "I don't understand where it goes."

"I don't know the details, but it gets burned up somehow in the process of making the talisman. He must keep just enough to sell a bit and bring back coins. But most of it is probably going straight to luck."

"So he's breaking the law, but we can't prove it, and we can't fight against it," Mevi summed up.

"And," Lina added, hesitant to reveal the next part, "there's one more thing. A side effect. Luckspinning works by taking a person's natural luck, capturing it, and amplifying it. So the owner of the talisman is really just expanding their own luck. But..."

Dedru sagged. "But in our case, it's taking our luck and giving it to Corym instead of us."

Lina winced in sympathy. "Unfortunately yes. Which I think must be another part of why everything you've tried goes badly. Your natural luck has been siphoned away."

"Then what can we do? Knowing he has actual, real luck on his side doesn't improve anything. If anything, it makes it worse. How do you fight against *good* luck when you have your own *bad* luck?"

That was the crux of the problem, of course.

"It's hopeless," Vira whispered.

"No," Seelah replied fiercely. "No situation is hopeless. We simply have to be more clever."

"Exactly," Lina added. "And now that you know what you're up against, you know how you have to go about it."

"We do?" asked Dedru.

"Yes. You have been fighting against Lord Corym directly, and at a disadvantage. Every move you've made has been in direct opposition to his goals and plans. You can't fight luck like that. With luck, you have to go at it sideways. You have to make it seem like you're fulfilling the needs of the luck magic, and you have to draw a trap."

"So we have to seem to be doing exactly what Lord Corym wants," Dedru said slowly, thinking through the implications, "until we spring something on him that the luck can't fight?"

"Exactly," Seelah said. "And it will help if Lina and I act out as much of the plan as possible, since we still have our own luck."

"Maybe the children too? They work for him, but they're not involved in the textiles."

"It will be dangerous though," Seelah warned.

Mevi snorted. "Dying slowly of starvation is also dangerous."

Vira patted Mevi's arm. "We'll ask them and let them decide."

Lina nodded. "That would help. Now, what does your lord want, more than anything?"

"Recognition," said Jhissa.

"To be drawn into higher circles."

"Out of this town."

"I think you're right, all of this. So we have to make him think there's a way to get what he wants."

"Are we sure we want to do this? What if it works and makes everything worse?"

"We won't lie to you," Seelah said. "It might. But do you have a better idea?"

No one had an answer for that.

"Then let's make Lord Corym's dreams come true."

They spent several minutes offering suggestions until suddenly Vira said, "Oh, I know! The hunt! The hunt is coming up."

There was a general murmur of excitement.

"Explain please," Lina asked.

Apparently there was a yearly event in the area, a hunt, where a number of local nobility gathered to socialize, to make alliances, and of course to hunt.

"The location changes every year, and I know Corym wants it here," Jhissa said. "It would raise his standing and bring him into contact with others who could change his fortunes."

Lina nodded, thinking. "Good. That should work."

"But we don't have a way of bringing it here," Dedru pointed out.

Lina sat back. She'd known it might come to this, trying to make an ally of an opponent. In fact, she suspected they'd be relying on him quite a bit before this plan was through. But that was always the nature of risk and reward. "I think I might have a way, but I'll need something else from you first. Does anyone in town have just a hint of fae blood?"

Tozo wasn't sure how much longer he would stay here, watching the two women. They were certainly hiding things, and he knew at least some of what they hid. But hiding was not a crime. Just because their secrets were more intriguing than most didn't mean he would follow them endlessly.

Especially if it kept him in places like this. It wasn't just the meager, poorly cooked food and the bad ale. He was used to that sort of thing in his travels. It was more the general weatherbeaten air of gloom here in town. As yet, he hadn't discovered its source, and it was likely outside his purview, but... it wasn't the kind of place you wanted to linger.

They'd been here over a week now, and other than roaming the town, talking to and meeting everyone, it didn't seem they'd done much else. There had been some sort of incident with the lord yesterday—Lord Corym, a young fellow Tozo hadn't seen yet. Something about an accident with his horse. He'd heard that the women were nearby, but as far as he could tell, it wasn't their doing, and purposeful violence didn't square with what he knew of them.

Tozo sat at his table in the corner of the little tavern, eating the underseasoned chicken and wilted greens he'd been served. Vestus was off fending for himself as he generally was when Tozo was in town. It made it easier to pass as a regular traveler if a trained morhawk didn't show up with him. But part of Tozo was jealous of his bird's freedom.

The door to the tavern opened, and Tozo raised an eyebrow. It was the women themselves. The tall one carried herself gracefully despite the cane she leaned on. The shorter one seemed to have a perpetual cheery grin, like a doting grandmother. They were a mismatched pair, but there was something to appreciate about them as well.

They stood in the doorway for a moment, looking around the room. The tall one saw him first and pointed. They headed straight for him.

"Greetings, truthseer," the tall one said.

He tipped his head. "Greetings, wanderers."

"I'm Lina, and this is Seelah. You may as well know, as you've been following us for three towns now." No dissembling here. Tozo appreciated someone who laid out the cards.

"I am Tozo," he said impassively. "At your service."

Lina snorted. "No, clearly not. But we think your following us has gone on long enough."

The plump one—Seelah—interrupted with a sheepish smile. "Now, Lina dear, don't be so unpleasant. The poor fellow is just doing his job." She looked down, almost like she was embarrassed, but he highly doubted that. "We'd like to confess so you can stop wasting your time and move on."

"I'm listening." He gestured to the bench across from him, and they sat. Seelah put a small basket on the table, and he caught a whiff of something delicious—especially after the cooking in this tavern.

"It's a little embarrassing," she said, "but not illegal. I've got a bit of fae blood in me, see. Nonspecific magic, just a knack for a few things." She lowered her voice. "Apparently my mother's mother's mother was a bit wild." She giggled.

He grunted noncommittally.

"I can make a delicious biscuit from just about anything," she continued, opening her basket. "But I don't have enough magic to do much of anything else. You must have noticed me baking with my cousins in their shop. We all have a touch, and maybe it was more than it should have been. Still, nothing funny happened." She gave a little self-deprecatory laugh as she handed him a small parcel wrapped in a napkin. "Except the most delicious cake I've ever tasted. This"—she gestured to the parcel—"isn't quite as good, but still I think you'll like it."

He unwrapped the parcel. Inside was a small pastry of some sort. It had the tiniest aura of fae magic to go with its sweet aroma. "You expect me to eat this?"

"You don't have to, of course." She shrugged and took another of the pastries from her basket and bit into it.

"Hmmm," he said. What an interesting story. But why were they bringing it to him now?

As if in answer to his question, Lina spoke up. "We didn't really want to explain it. People tend to get suspicious when Seelah tells them she has fae blood. You know how it is, with the old prejudices."

She wasn't wrong. That was part of why his job existed—so the humans could see that the fae took peace and lawkeeping seriously.

"We thought you'd get bored of following us since Seelah doesn't do anything interesting. So we didn't want to fuss, but now..." She paused. "We've found something much bigger. We think you'll want to check it out, and we're hoping that afterward you'll choose to leave us alone."

He very much doubted there was anything more interesting than what he'd seen in these women since he began following them, but he was willing to hear. "What have you found?"

"A luckspinner."

He shrugged. Nothing unusual about that. They weren't exactly common, but they weren't worth looking into.

"No," Lina said. "I'm not done. A luckspinner who's spinning luck for the wrong person. Has been for two years now, massive amounts of it." She sat back, looking satisfied.

As well she might. That was indeed much bigger than anything they'd told him about themselves. "Are you sure?"

They exchanged a quick glance before Seelah answered. "I saw his talisman tarnish."

He raised an eyebrow. "How did you manage that?"

She grinned. "I guess I just had my own moment of luck."

"Hmmm," he said. Even looking straight at a luckspun talisman was difficult for most people. He glanced between the two women. He had a sneaking suspicion it was Lina who'd seen it, not Seelah. Again, interesting that they kept throwing Seelah into the light and casting Lina into the background. Not surprising though, all things considered. But he would go along with their efforts, as much as they wanted. For now.

"Will you investigate?" Seelah asked, her hands clasped.

He blew out a breath. If what they were telling him was true, the luckspinner was violating both ancient mores and also the laws established between human and fae. Both the man and the fae were in a great deal of trouble. "Yes, but as you likely know, luckspinning is challenging to catch, even for someone like me." Luckspinners were notoriously slippery, even when they weren't breaking the law. If they *were* breaking the law, it would be much harder to catch them.

"We have a suggestion for you on that. I assume you need some sort of evidence to bring him to justice?" Lina asked.

Tozo nodded. "The evidence of my sight is enough for a hearing, but I will need more tangible evidence to end things."

"Then send that morhawk of yours with a message. You need to change the location of the local hunt. Have them come here."

"And this will reveal the luckspinner and the lordling?"

Lina smiled. "We have a plan."

The meeting with the truthseer—Tozo—had gone well, Lina thought. Most fae in his position took justice very seriously, and he'd clearly been bothered by the idea of the illicit luckspinning. He seemed to believe the story of themselves as well. At least he'd certainly enjoyed the treat that Seelah and Mevi's cousin had made.

Hopefully the bit of fae in the cousin's blood had shown up in the food. Since truthseers were known to sense the presence of fae magic but not where it came from, he wouldn't sense the lie in Seelah's story. They were safe there, and hopefully they'd given him sufficient explanation for any sense of the fae he'd seen around them. And hopefully something far more exciting to pay attention to than two boring old women with nothing else to hide.

It wasn't a perfect plan, but it was a hope, and Lina could work with that.

In the next days, Tozo quickly set to work on his part of the deal. The town was abuzz with news that the hunt was coming.

Lord Corym put his servants to work, including the children who were supposedly learning. He told them preparing for and seeing the nobility—from a respectable and invisible distance, of course—would be an educational opportunity for their future positions. What those future positions were to be, he did not say, but he did enlist them to straighten the manor house, dust out every cobweb, polish and re-polish everything to a perfect shine.

Which suited Lina's plan just fine. Because by now, the older children had begun to realize that the lord's "education" was not what he'd promised. They saw their families afraid, in poverty, getting more desperate by the day. They were ready to help. And they still had their own luck.

So if a staircase was waxed just a little too perfectly, Lord Corym might slip. No injury, of course, but just a tiny bit of luck leached away.

And if one of the kitchen staff suggested that Corym should keep the wine flowing late into the night because the other nobility would be impressed at the wealth it displayed, that same staff member would remember to water everyone else's wine, as was custom. But it might just slip her mind that Lord Corym's should be watered too. And drunkenness had never made the lordling's personality particularly appealing, so he might drain off luck simply in avoiding being seen as a buffoon.

Those were the satisfying types of tricks they planned, but mostly their efforts would have to be more subtle. As the glittering crowd trickled in to celebrate the hunt, everyone involved in the plan carefully sought ways to use Lord Corym's luck as much as possible, as innocently as possible. They wanted it out by the last night of the hunt.

Too direct an effort was likely to backfire—like the powdered twitchwort that Corym's valet sprinkled in his clothing. It was meant to cause itch and irritation, showing him to disadvantage, but somehow it also gained the lordling the sympathy of a young, unmarried noble lady who could be a highly desirable match.

On the other hand, too indirect and it might not use his good luck at all.

So mostly they encouraged him in exactly what he wanted—to show off his extravagance, to impress the nobles who could help him in his social climb.

The servants set about boasting to the various nobility about the glories of Dryss, the excellent textiles, the thriving village, the marvelous education they were receiving. All exhibitions of prosperity, except that, aside from the fabric, not one of the claims had any evidence. Surely the nobility would notice the disparity and be unimpressed with Lord Corym's management of his people.

His valet idly told him one night that he'd heard a lady complaining about the length of the hunt. It was too short, she said, not enough time to really enjoy Lord Corym's generous hospitality.

The next day he declared the hunt would continue an additional week.

Maybe for many nobles, it would not be a challenge to host a group of this size for two weeks instead of one. But for Corym and his town of Dryss, it would be challenging.

The food would run lower and lower, even as the cook scrambled to import extra supplies. The wine would be increasingly watered, all except Corym's.

The true evil of a two-week celebration, however, was in the lordling himself. His personality. His laugh that was a touch too loud, a touch too long. His endless dwelling on his own self-importance. Two weeks was time for Corym to sap his own luck simply in keeping his guests from dreading every interaction.

That was the plan at least. It was delicate and fueled largely by hope and desperation.

The days passed, but still everything he touched seemed to turn for his benefit. His luck had not run down enough, and the final night of the hunt was approaching.

It was pure chance that Tozo saw when the luckspinner came back to town. He'd set aside the obvious accouterments of his profession—sending Vestus off again after he'd arranged for the hunt's relocation—and spent most of his time the last few days blending in with the minor nobility. Too important to be uninvited, not important enough to be worth paying much attention. Just how he liked it.

The women had been right about Lord Corym. He'd seen the man's talisman rings and pendants the moment they met, despite the heavy glamour that hid them. He'd expected the women to be right, of course, but it really was a flagrant violation of the law.

Tozo lounged in the gardens at a picnic with various of the other nobles. His body was in the garden, but his mind wandered back to Lina and Seelah. Who were they really? Who was Lina, and was she dangerous to the kingdom's safety? That's all he had to know for sure. She could be whatever she wanted, hide whatever she wished, as long as she did not intend harm.

In all he'd seen from either of the women so far, there had been little desire for conflict, but even with her walking stick, Lina moved like she'd trained for battle once upon a long time ago. She was old enough to have been recruited to the war, just a few years before he was. Had she been there?

The clatter of a wagon over at the stables drew his attention. And once he'd seen the wagon driver, he could almost pay attention to nothing else. He had his suspicions about Lina, but that mystery would have to wait.

Different magics were noticeable in different ways. Some were subtle and soft, a sort of light sparkle. Others were showy and bright, colorful and chaotic. The luckspinner—his magic was the gaudy kind. Training had honed Tozo's sight to a level most truthseers never achieved, but even the dullest of truthseers would notice the luckspinner's garishness. Strange that the magic that was so obvious to a truthseer was so forgettable to others.

All this Tozo thought as the fae jumped down from his seat, handed the reins to a stablehand, and entered the manor house.

Tozo sat up. His arrival was unfortunate. They'd hoped Lord Corym would be too foolish to notice how quickly he was running through his luck and perhaps he wouldn't send for the luckspinner before the end.

They hadn't counted on it, though, given Corym's obsession with his own image. Of course he took careful inventory of every moment and every drop of luck, and of course he would do his best not to run out—including calling in his friend to spin him new talismans.

Ah well, he was here now, so the women would simply have to work harder to drain the lord's luck. And if the situation got desperate, Tozo himself would help, though it would be better if he was not directly involved.

He stood abruptly, and the conversation around him halted for a moment. "My apologies," he said, bowing politely to the others. "I have just remembered an urgent matter I must attend to."

He strode from the garden, considering the best way to reach Lina and let her know the luckspinner had returned.

Lina watched from a shadow as Seelah approached the group of noblewomen.

"Milady," Seelah called to one of them, a lovely woman on a black mare, wearing a riding habit in the height of fashion.

The woman stopped, and Seelah stepped forward, holding out an exquisite skirt. "A gift for you, milady, from the town." She gave a quick curtsy and held out the clothing.

It was made from the finest linen the town had to offer, a deep, soft crimson covered in embroidery and sewn primarily by Seelah late into the night all week.

There were better seamstresses in Dryss, but none that would be untouched by the leaching of luck, so they'd decided it was best if Seelah did as much of the work as possible. Lina stayed away from the task; she was not the ideal option for any sewing that was meant to be presentable.

The lady took one look at the clothing and swiftly dismounted to gather the cloth in her hands, stroking it with practiced fingers. "The weave is beautiful. And this red, it almost glows." She looked at Seelah with a broad smile. "I thank you and the town. Is this your handiwork?"

Seelah curtsied again. "Yes, milady, but I am far from the finest seamstress here."

The lady continued her appreciation of the skirt, holding it up to the light, rubbing her fingers along the cloth.

"The fabric would make a beautiful full bodice as well, milady," Seelah prompted.

"Yes, it would. How much do you have? I would like to purchase it."

Seelah looked down. "Oh, well, you'll have to speak to Lord Corym about that. His trader takes all our cloth and sells it at market. I gave him some just this morning."

It had been a single bolt. The luckspinner had come yesterday in a foul mood, demanding any wares that any of the townspeople had saved up, but excuses came aplenty. Mysterious stains on the fabric. A contagious cough that had laid out a whole spinning family so nothing had been produced since last month. One woman finally offered the single beautiful bolt of red.

They hadn't wanted to give the lordling anything at all. But as with all of this, it was a balancing act of appeasing the luck just enough to continue setting the trap. Corym would be getting another talisman, but in letting him take just one small bit of luck, they hoped to force him into using far more—hopefully all he had left.

"I hear he's leaving tomorrow morning to trade it away. You'll have to speak with him before then," Seelah added.

The lady tilted her head. "Oh, I suppose I'll have to," she said, but there was little conviction in it. Had she already lost interest?

"The color is perfect for your skin," Seelah prodded, "if you don't mind my saying, milady."

She looked again at the fabric, and Lina smiled. They'd heard she was not only supremely fashionable but also very vain.

"You're right. I must have some. Thank you again," she said, and she called to a groom to help her remount her horse.

Lina came out of the shadows to stand beside Seelah as the lady rode away. "Well done. The trap is as ready as we can make it. Now it's for that truthseer to nudge his quarry in and spring it."

Seelah grinned. "He'll do a fine job, I've no doubt."

Lina smiled too, but still she worried. They had hoped to keep the luckspinner away. Barring that, they'd hoped for some material sign that Lord Corym's luck was running low. The trader's anger and desperation for goods was a hopeful sign at least. They would have to wait and see.

Tozo moved through the bright throng of nobles silently, always near the edges of the crowd. He watched their exchanges and laughter. He watched the way they moved with the grace born of self-assurance.

He watched Lord Corym, who, Tozo could tell, was not so sure of himself. He had a hunger about him that revealed itself in all he did. It made him commit little errors of manners, push just a bit too hard when he should have only nudged, nudge when he should have pulled back.

Most of all, though, Tozo watched the ring on his finger slowly tarnish as he made error after error. Tozo felt a smug sort of satisfaction that Corym was even now, through all his missteps and his general obnoxious personality, bringing himself closer and closer to failure.

The night wore on, and Lord Corym left the hall and returned with different jewelry three times. The luckspinner was here, squirreled away in a nearby room. Tozo had set guards to linger nearby—not to capture him yet, as they had nothing to charge him with, but just to be ready.

Time was running out though. The nobles would disperse to their rooms soon. The lordling moved nervously, glancing at the ring on his finger more than once. It still shone, but more dully than before.

Tozo would have to risk it.

He approached the noblewoman who'd received the skirt from Seelah. "Milady," he whispered, "didn't I hear you wanted to ask Lord Corym about his people's fine cloth?"

She looked up from her glass of wine. "Yes, indeed. Gorgeous stuff, must have it." But she remained seated and took another sip.

"Perhaps now would be a good time. You might forget tomorrow in the bustle of leaving. It would be such a shame to miss out."

She nodded. "It would." Then she paused. "But now is not the time. I'll ask Lord Corym tomorrow, or I'll write to him. There's no rush."

"I thought they said this particular pattern was one of a kind?" he ventured. They'd probably said no such thing, but he needed to get her moving.

She turned fully to face him. "Who did you say you were?" Her voice was suspicious now. "And why do you care?"

Tozo had to back down. Pushing too hard would not help the cause. "Just a friend," he said. "I thought you wanted to buy the fabric. My mistake." He turned away and faded into the crowd before she could ask more questions.

The ring still shone. They hadn't done enough.

He could move on to the next part of the plan. He'd always been meant to question the upstart lordling in this public forum, this last night of the hunt. He'd always been meant to out the man's behavior in a place where there were too many witnesses to sweep under the rug. But he'd also been meant to do it after the lordling had no luck left.

If the noblewoman had stood up and asked Lord Corym about the fabric, Tozo was certain he could have led the conversation, discovering to everyone present that the bolt of fabric—which Corym should have easily been able to produce—had disappeared. The conversation would have drained vast quantities of luck as the lordling tried to explain the inexplicable.

Since that hadn't worked, he'd have to hazard beginning the interrogation while the dregs of luck remained. It might get cut short. Corym might be able to slip out of the noose, though Tozo couldn't think of how. But that was the tricky thing about luck—you couldn't really guess how it might manifest. He'd much prefer if it was gone before he began.

Lina had told him they had a last-ditch plan in case they hadn't managed to leach away the lordling's luck or in case the lady could not be convinced into a confrontation, and Tozo had observed a few of the townspeople acting as servants, waiting for a signal. But he had no idea what the last-ditch plan was. Laughter and dancing and merriment surrounded him, but all he could do was scan the room, waiting.

Maybe he would have to take another step himself. Lord Corym still had the dregs of luck in his current ring, so Tozo would have to be careful. But if he could drain it through some sort of public embarrassment or danger, then he could proceed with the public revelation.

He just had to come up with a suitable plan.

An object flew through the air, straight toward Lord Corym's head.

A gasp rose from a few in the crowd, and then, impossibly, the object slid just past the side of his head, bounced off a pillar behind him, and fell to the ground with a heavy thud. Tozo eyed the object—a large, solid pewter pitcher. It had been on a perfect collision course, and based on the murmurs in the crowd, he was not the only one who'd noticed.

Tozo glanced quickly to Corym's ring. Its final shine was gone. It was time to strike.

Red-faced, Corym spun in the direction the pitcher had come from. "Who did that?" he roared.

Everyone on that end of the room looked around for the culprit. A young woman with dark hair stood defiantly still.

"Guards!" Corym yelled. "Arrest her!"

Within moments, three guards had dashed into the room, caught the young woman, and dragged her toward Lord Corym. The crowd made space around them.

"Who are you?" Corym demanded.

"My name is Mevi," she replied, her voice bold.

"Do you know the punishment for assaulting a lord?"

"I don't care." She stood tall, and if she was afraid, it didn't show.

"Take her away and lock her up," Corym said.

"Wait!" Tozo stepped forward. "I believe we should question her first. Make sure there are no other plots against you."

Corym looked nervously down at his ring. "The guards can question her on their own. They don't need you to make it happen."

"Ah, but I think I can save them some time in gathering evidence for justice." Tozo took his papers out and showed them to Lord Corym. "I am a truthseer."

Corym gaped and surreptitiously hid his hand behind his back. "Fine. Go with the guards and question her."

Tozo shook his head. "No, I believe I should do it here." He turned toward this Mevi woman, clearly the plan Lina had mentioned.

She held her head high and said nothing. Yet.

"Tell us, Mevi," Tozo said, his voice carrying around the room. "Why have you assaulted your lord?"

"He is not *my* lord. He should not be anyone's. He has destroyed our town and our spirits, and I only wish the pitcher had hit him the way it should have if he weren't using magic."

A murmur swept the room then.

"What do you mean?" Tozo asked, as if he didn't know the answer.

"He's been taking every bit of cloth and thread and yarn we make here and using it to spin his own luck. While we're starving and dying, he's currying favor with all of you." Her eyes swept the room, and though she was only a commoner and they were nobility, she seemed to think it was they who were beneath her, not the other way around.

"What proof do you have?"

"You mean besides the evidence that you must be able to see, as a truthseer? There's his jewelry—that ring on his hand, whatever else he has in his rooms. And the trader that comes and pretends he's selling our wares. That's the luckspinner who helps him."

The murmurs in the room got louder, and Tozo could see that finally the glamour on the jewelry was fading. Throughout the room, here and there, a noble would shake their head and try to glimpse Corym's ring—which he still hid behind his back. Eyes filled with confusion and concern. The crowd pressed in, closing off any avenue of escape for the young lord.

Tozo turned to him and raised his voice again. "What do you have to say for yourself? And before you answer, remember that I am a truthseer and that your ring's luck seems to have run out."

Corym glanced involuntarily at his hand then opened his mouth, but no words emerged.

A smile slowly spread across Tozo's face. "Yes, that's what I thought." He caught sight of the miller's daughter, the one Lina and Seelah had been working with, standing at the edge of the room, acting as one of the servants.

She stared straight at him, ready.

"Is there anyone else with something to say?" Tozo asked.

The young woman stepped forward immediately. "My name is Dedru. I have testimony against this man." And she explained the months of struggle under Corym's rule, the deaths of her brothers the previous winter, and her father's beating. "He did not kill my brothers, but everything else is a result of what he has done to our town."

Tozo nodded solemnly. "Anyone else?"

Another young woman stepped forward with a story about her brother and sister working for Corym with little hope of advancement or freedom.

And then another young woman.

Then an older man who, from his resemblance to the first woman, had to be the miller. He hobbled forward to tell the story of being robbed and left for dead.

Then an older lady, who spoke of weaving for a lord who no longer paid enough to keep a roof over her head.

Another.

Another.

With each voice, Corym seemed to shrink a little more, and the townspeople grew, expanded, releasing the suffering they'd experienced under this man's rule. The nobles around them seemed to feel the weight of the testimonies. They were not perfect, but few of them would have hatched such a scheme and hurt their own people like this.

It was enough to make Tozo's blood boil.

Finally the last voice testified, and there was silence.

And in that silence, Tozo realized something: the guards were here, now holding Corym's arms, determined to keep him from escape. But if the guards were here, who was watching the luckspinner's room?

Tozo pulled a small whistle from his pocket and blew.

This was the part of the plan that Lina hated. The part where she could do so little. She and Seelah and the women had done all they could to drain the lordling's luck, and she hoped the townspeople were even now taking back the power their lord had stolen. But Lina and Seelah themselves had to wait while the truthseer gathered the final evidence.

Lina could not be seen by the hunting group. Even standing in the shadows of the stable was risky, with so many nobles up in the manor house. There was a chance—a slim one, but still a chance—that someone would recognize her from the time of the treaty. But the odds were good that no aristocrat would wander into the stables while the party and the food and the wine were inside. If someone did come, she would hide.

She had meant to stay back at the mill and wait for news, wait to see if their plan had worked. But she hadn't been able to force herself to keep away. She leaned on her walking stick and waited.

A soft sound from the door sent her deeper into the shadows. What was it? The sound came again, unmistakable this time—a surreptitious footfall. Lina stayed still and waited.

A form appeared in the stable's doorway, outlined by the moonlight filtering in from outside. The form moved stealthily but with haste. He turned and froze, as if to listen for something, and in that same bit of moonlight, Lina saw his face.

It was the luckspinner.

Why was he here? Tozo was supposed to keep both the lord and the luckspinner inside. If one was out here, had something gone wrong? Lina's mind raced.

Her grip on her walking stick tightened as she considered. Perhaps the first part of the trap had been sprung, but now this quarry was trying to evade the hunt. Or perhaps they had failed altogether, and Lord Corym was free as well.

Either way, she could do nothing about the lordling up in his manor, but she could at least make sure the luckspinner found justice.

She stepped out of the shadows. "Good evening, sir," she said.

The luckspinner jumped, startled, and dropped the harness he'd been taking down. "Good evening."

"You aren't back there in the festivities. Why not?" She shuffled forward casually, moving closer to him.

"Just out for a breath of air." He noted her lower-class clothing, her aged body, her cane, and sniffed. "Not that it is any of your business."

She paused for a moment. They hadn't spent much time worrying about the spinner's stored luck. They'd assumed it would be siphoned away sufficiently with the lordling's. The prevailing theory, based on his behaviors in town, was that the spinner had no great ambitions or subtle use for the luck he gained—he seemed to want only an easy life, little work, unearned comforts, and safety from consequences. That should have been sufficiently siphoned by now. But if he also had some other, greater desire—skills with weapons, powerful muscles—well, Lina was about to find out.

"Ah, but it *is* my business," she said, and she slid forward.

It had been years since Lina had participated in full-on combat, but she never let herself get out of practice. She'd sparred with imaginary partners in her little cottage at night. She'd learned how to use her blacksmith hammer for both creativity and destruction. And most recently, she'd spent hours converting a harmless walking stick into a swift cudgel. It wasn't an elegant weapon, but she didn't need elegance.

She lifted the wood into both hands and shifted her weight, enjoying the stick's heft.

The luckspinner barely had time to widen his eyes in surprise at her sudden change before she swung—first at his neck, and then, with a quick adjustment, driving the stick into his abdomen.

He bent over under the onslaught, gasping and reaching for something inside his jacket even as he tried to catch his breath.

She swung again, this time striking him on the side of the head.

He fell to the ground and lay still, his hand loosing to drop the knife he'd pulled from his jacket. Lina stood watching him for a moment, ready to swing again if necessary, but he appeared unconscious. It wouldn't last—she didn't think she'd hit him hard enough for long-term damage—but it gave her a moment at least.

Perhaps if he hadn't underestimated her, it would have been more of a fight, but as it was, Lina was left barely breathing hard and strangely disappointed at the ease of subduing him.

Unfortunately, she did still need to keep him contained. She looked around the stable for something to tie him up with.

"Need help?"

Lina didn't bother to turn. She just nodded, and Seelah appeared in her peripheral vision. "How'd you know?"

"I had a sneaking suspicion you wouldn't be able to stay away," she said, bustling forward with a length of rope.

Lina shrugged guiltily.

Seelah knelt and picked up the knife, holding it out with an expression of distaste. "You should take care of this."

Lina nodded and took it carefully, holding the blade edge rather than the wrought iron handle.

Seelah winced. "Oh, sorry, I didn't think of that."

Lina shrugged. "No matter," she said as she slipped the knife into her pocket.

Seelah made short work of tight knots around the spinner's ankles as Lina hovered over them with her cane, ready for further violence if he began to stir. Another minute, and his hands were bound as well.

Seelah stood again and brushed the dust from her hands. "Not much of a fighter?"

Lina shook her head. "Extremely unimpressive."

It was Seelah's turn to look around. "Should we find a guard or a soldier or someone?"

It would be better not to get involved further, but they couldn't just leave him there, could they?

A high-pitched screech came from outside the stable, and in a rush of feathers, the truthseer's morhawk flew into the room and landed on a post.

They eyed each other.

Lina gestured to the luckspinner on the ground. "I believe this is what you're looking for."

The bird cocked its head to the side, then flew over to land on the unconscious fae, talons digging into the exposed skin.

Lina nodded in satisfaction. "That should do it, don't you think?"

Seelah agreed. "Let's get back home and have a snack before bed."

Lina and Seelah sat quietly at the kitchen table as Dedru and Seftin described all that had happened the night before—that the lordling was revealed and swiftly imprisoned, that there would be equally swift justice, that the luckspinner was also imprisoned, though under somewhat more mysterious circumstances.

Lina smiled at that.

"Seeing that wretch stripped of his title?" Dedru smiled. "That's going to give me years of happy memories."

"I'm just glad we could be part of it." Seftin rose from his seat and winced. "I thank you, but I admit that last night and this morning have worn me out. If you'll forgive me, I'll be back to bed now."

Lina and Seelah said their goodbyes as Dedru helped him walk slowly, stiffly back to his room.

For that matter, Lina was moving a little stiffly this morning as well. She must have pulled a muscle. So much for last night being too easy.

At the sound of hooves on the path outside, Lina and Seelah rose. They'd been expecting this visit.

"I'm sure you've already heard," Tozo said when Seelah opened the door to greet him.

"That Lord Corym and the trader are both contained?" Seelah asked. "Of course, since practically half the town was there."

Tozo nodded. "An excellent turnout for the event."

"We thank you for your efforts," Lina said, gesturing him inside. "It could not have happened without you."

"I thank you for bringing the matter to my attention. As you suggested, it will be lucrative for me, and it's good to keep such behaviors from becoming commonplace."

"Believe me, it was our pleasure."

Seelah headed to the kitchen. "Let me get some cake."

"It's interesting, though," Tozo continued as he sat in a chair across from Lina. "I contained Lord Corym inside the manor, but the luckspinner was able to sneak out."

"Oh?" Lina asked.

"Yes. I admit to a bit of embarrassment there. I should have had him watched more closely."

"We all make mistakes."

"Yes," he said slowly, looking around the room. His eyes fell on the walking stick by the front door, and a satisfied smile spread across his face. "Yes. But fortunately, someone was able to stop him. I found him in the stable, trussed like a pig for the spit. I'd called Vestus back in the hopes he could locate the fae, but apparently it wasn't needed. Vestus was simply watching over him, and the spinner wouldn't say how he got that way."

Lina shrugged. "I can't imagine."

"No, I'm sure you can't."

"What happens next?"

"Corym will be brought to the king for judgment. The luckspinner... he'll be dealt with by the fae court. He won't be heard from again for a long time, if ever."

Lina winced. He would deserve the punishment, yes, but the fae court was not known for its gentleness.

"And Dryss?"

"I'll report to the king, then come back here to help reestablish order and advise on who should take over. We'll make sure they're in good hands. I'll be quite busy for a while."

That was taken care of then. "And... what do you intend to do regarding Seelah?"

Tozo raised an eyebrow. "Regarding Seelah? Nothing. Her fae blood is of little import." He watched her for a moment, as if waiting for her to reveal something.

She would not be revealing anything.

"I was thinking," he said. "About the war."

Lina blinked. "Oh?"

"Yes. I noticed you and I are nearly of an age. Were you recruited into battle?"

She shrugged, hoping to play it off. "I was, briefly. I'm afraid I wasn't much of a fighter."

He cocked that disbelieving eyebrow again. "I doubt that."

She shrugged again, but his piercing gaze was unnerving, and she struggled to remain nonchalant.

"I wonder, Lina-wanderer. What is it that you care about? What set you to wandering?"

Where was this conversation going? She didn't know, but here at least she could tell the truth. "I care about justice. I care about peace."

He looked at her in silence for a few moments then nodded once. "I believe you. And thank you, you have answered another question that I feared I would not find the answer to."

"I have?"

"You have."

"And will you leave us alone now?"

"It seems only fair. As you say, you haven't been doing anything I should worry about."

"And we will not. We seek only to be left alone."

"I believe that." Tozo unfolded his frame from the seat and bowed before leaning in and lowering his voice. "I would like to offer you a suggestion, however."

"Yes?"

"I do not wish to boast, but I am a more powerful truthseer than most."

Lina swallowed.

"Anyone with enough of the skill to be called a truthseer can, of course, recognize when someone is using magic."

Lina knew this.

"We can tell if an object is infused with magic."

Which was how they knew he'd be able to see the talismans, even with their protective glamour. Lina nodded uneasily.

"And a very few of us can sense the magic's mere existence, whether it is being used or not." He stared pointedly at her.

Lina's heart beat wildly. He knew about her.

But how much did he know?

"You needn't fear, Lina-wanderer—at least you needn't fear me." He looked her straight in the eye and spoke clearly, distinctly. A declaration.

An oath.

"I will not share what I know about you, or about your friend. All of your secrets are safe with me. I swear it."

Lina felt the words wash over her, felt the binding take effect. She relaxed, and the warmth of gratitude washed through her as well. "Thank you."

He nodded sincerely. "But remember I am not the only truth-seer around. Very few have the sight that I have, but not none. If I were you, I'd avoid any place you see a morhawk about."

Lina nodded back. "We will be more careful."

He smiled then, and the smile made him far more attractive than he had been in all their acquaintance up to now. "Good."

Seelah bustled back into the room, a large square of something bundled in a brown cloth napkin. "Here you go," she said, breaking the tension in the room. "Some cake for you, made by Dedru. It won't keep for more than a day or two, so don't you waste it."

Seelah, of course, had been the one to make it, but she didn't know Tozo already knew all their secrets—including that Lina was the true fae, not Seelah.

Tozo turned to her with that same smile. "Seelah-wanderer, you are a treasure." He unwrapped the cake to breathe in its warm aroma, closing his eyes in pleasure. "And so modest too, pretending Dedru made the cake. But I recognize that hint of the fae in it." He rewrapped the napkin and placed it carefully in his satchel.

Seelah stood frozen, but her eyes darted to Lina.

Lina looked back and began to laugh. "A hint of the fae." She shook her head. "I can't believe it."

Tozo's brow furrowed. "You mean, you didn't know?"

Seelah continued frozen.

Lina finally answered. "We didn't. Of course I always knew her food was delicious, but we made up the story about her fae blood to throw you off about... other things."

Tozo chuckled too then. "The two of you just get more and more interesting the more I know about you."

Seelah finally snapped out of her shock. "I hope not interesting enough to follow us again?" she ventured.

"No, you're safe there. Although I wouldn't mind crossing your paths again someday. You and Lina are lucky—" He winced. "Maybe I will not say lucky. You are both blessed in your traveling companions. Take care of each other."

"We always do," Seelah said, regaining more of her equilibrium. "Now be on your way. We're sure you have places to be."

"I do indeed, and my bird is getting restless." With a quick wave, he exited the house.

Lina watched him go for a moment, her mind still reeling from the fear, the relief, the revelations of the past minutes.

It was strange. So many years of hiding alone, keeping her secret alone. But Seelah had joined her and been a gift in the solitude. Seelah had helped to keep her safe. And now this Tozo—an unexpected secret keeper as well. Alone was not turning out to be the only way to survive.

Then the obvious occurred to her. She followed him outside and called out. "Tozo, wait!"

He turned.

"I don't know who has heard it, but there is another... matter that needs addressing." She told him briefly of Tyblith and the torque and the mindturning. "I don't know where they are now. Information was sent, but I couldn't follow up."

He nodded, his eyes bright with thought and perhaps a spark of anticipation for the potential danger. "Thank you. I hadn't heard. Which in itself is worrisome. Something of that import should have set all of us on alert. I will look into it. I swear it."

She nodded at the binding. "Good."

"Good."

Lina watched him mount his horse then whistle into the sky. A few moments later, the morhawk dove down and landed on Tozo's shoulder. He patted the bird and clicked to his horse.

Seelah stood at the counter when Lina returned inside, packing goods into a basket. She seemed to have completely gotten over the discovery of her fae blood. "Well? Is everything all right?"

Lina nodded. "It is."

"Then what shall we do next?"

"It will be interesting to find out, don't you think?"

Sharp and Pointy Teeth

THE SUN FILTERING THROUGH the leaves of the trees above me cast shafts of light through to the undergrowth. It would have been really quite lovely if I weren't running for my life.

I hopped over a fallen log, dodged under a branch, and cursed at the trees grabbing at my long hair streaming behind me as I ran. Noises followed me—the loud, crashing sound of George as he stumbled after me, trying to keep up, of course. But also the softer, more ominous rustling of something *large* sliding after us. I hadn't caught more than a glimpse of it, so all I knew was that it was pale brown, and vast, and dangerous. The rows and rows of sharp, pointy teeth were kind of a giveaway.

"What did you say it was?" I called over my shoulder to George as we ran through the forest. I had to have misunderstood him. "I thought you called it Bitey Box."

George panted and huffed. "Yeah," he yelled, "you heard right." I glanced back to see him duck under the same branch I'd dodged, trying not to lose his footing. I was already going slowly to let him keep up, but he was slowing down even further. At this rate, the monster would catch us long before we could make it out of the forest.

I turned and kept going, my mind racing, seeking a solution. I'd left all my weaponry in the coat closet under the hockey gear. I guess this is what I got for assuming I could spend a day just picnicking and having fun with friends.

Then again, who could have predicted an evil sorcerer appearing in the meadow and summoning a monster from the deepest abysses of time and space on the very same day that I was there to eat burgers and slightly stale chips?

And who really could have predicted that it would be named Bitey Box?

Still, I should have been ready. And now I was running for my life, trying to save George, and wondering what exactly we were even running *from*.

Well, I wasn't going to leave my swords at home ever again, even on the days I volunteered for craft time at the kindergarten or worked my part-time job as a server at Big Sal's Pizza. I'd just have to disguise them as paintbrushes or spatulas or something.

But that was a problem for another day, a problem I would only have if I survived *this* day.

I paused in my running, willing George to hurry up. "Did you see what kind of a creature it is?" I'd been too busy trying to clear people away and then get out of there to notice.

"I think," he panted, "it might actually"—pant—"be a box"—pant pant—"or something." He paused and hopped over another fallen log. "But with teeth."

I guess that would explain the name.

What could we do? There were too many obstacles in the forest to make running easy, even though they didn't seem to be slowing down Bitey Box at all. And once we reached the edge of the forest—which was coming soon—we'd be in town. The mall was less than a mile away, the school even closer, and the library close by too. I didn't want to see how this beast would terrorize my little town. I had to *do* something.

A box, I thought. A big brown box. What kinds of weaknesses did a box have?

And that's when it hit me. "George," I yelled, looking over my shoulder to gauge how much Bitey Box had gained on us. "Follow me right! I have a plan."

"Right? Are you sure?" he called back.

"Yes!" I screamed, then sprinted toward the edge of the forest and the open space beyond.

I stood in the sunlight, squinting at the sudden brightness, bending over with my hands on my knees as I tried to catch my breath. Perfect. My sense of direction hadn't led me astray. I ran more slowly now, making sure Bitey Box didn't lose my scent or get distracted by another target.

I yanked open a door and sped through a quiet hallway lined with more doors, headed toward one I knew very well, covered in construction paper sheep and drawings of trees.

I tugged it open and practically fell into the room.

"Sarah," a chorus of voices shouted. "Sarah!" Twenty-three kindergarteners jumped up and surrounded me, hugging my legs.

I smiled at them and tried to hide my exhaustion.

The children kept running around in excitement and pelted me with questions about why I was there on the wrong day. I could barely think through the cacophony.

Just then, the monster slid through the doorway, coming into full view for the first time.

A sudden silence descended over the children as they stared, open-mouthed, at the beast.

I grinned. "I know it's not craft day," I said, bending to look into their eyes and lowering my voice to a whisper, "but I brought you something really special and I just couldn't wait."

The children cheered loudly.

I clapped. "Now who wants to get the scissors?"

A little girl waved her hand excitedly.

"Okay, Lily. You get the scissors. But remember—don't run with them. Safety first."

She nodded and rushed to the scissor box. She pulled out a single pair, and a ray of sunlight through the window sliced across the scissors, making them gleam like razor-sharp teeth. I turned to face Bitey Box. "You made a big mistake coming to this dimension, Bitey Box," I said.

Though you wouldn't think a sentient cardboard box could show much emotion, I swear I saw a shiver of fear cross its face.

An hour later I smiled, walking around the room and complimenting every child's project. "Really great cardboard castle there, Henry," I said. "I love how you've cut out little windows."

Henry beamed.

"And Akira, are those teeth you've used to create stalactites for your diorama? So clever!"

Akira nodded shyly.

I stood up and stretched, sighing happily to myself. Craft day at kindergarten was the best.

But I still planned to pack my swords next time.

To Dance with the Fae

First it's in my toes. A tiny shift, a desperate wiggle. I can't keep still. Toes were made to dance.

It's in my ankles next, then my knees and thighs and hips, shoulders, wrists, fingers. My cells vibrate to the sound.

There was a different sound before this, a sound I should probably remember. I chased it here, to this meadow, glowing in the sunlight under a vibrant blue sky.

A bark? My fingers close on emptiness; I should be holding something. A leash, I think. My dog's leash. He heard the music, he followed the sound. And I followed my dog.

Now the rhythmic ebb and flow is drowning out the noise of other thoughts. Is it drums? Flutes? Strings?

I sneak closer, just to learn the tune.

The dog will take care of himself... or I'll find him soon. After I whirl to the music for a minute or two.

Or three.

The beat is an aching itch, a bone-deep need to dance. The only relief is surrender. I fly, I spin, I soar. The harder I dance, the faster I whirl, the closer I come to scratching that itch. So close.

I've nearly gotten it, I think. Maybe. I need the relief so desperately.

Then, suddenly, someone else is there—tall, beautiful, stepping with perfect grace. He turns and pulls me into his rhythm, light on my feet, flying in time with the sound of my heartbeat, the brush of the music, the rush of his movement.

Another few minutes, really. Just until I figure out this part, this next step. Then I'll go... do whatever I'm supposed to be doing. I'll think about that soon, so soon.

Then—a voice I maybe recognize, coming from so far away. "Mom," it calls. "Mom!"

I want to answer, I do. But the rhythm pulls me away.

I shake my head. Later.

"Please," the voice calls, farther away this time. It jars against the song, a discordant chord. My step falters.

The man pulls me back into the steps. I look into his face. Had I looked before? It's handsome but somehow forgettable the moment I look away. I can't remember his eyes, the cut of his hair, the line of his jaw.

But there is only the dance now. Everything else is irrelevant.

Then I hear the voice again, a fierce whisper, breaking the waves of rhythm I've been traveling. "I need you," it begs. "Please."

I stumble again as its notes interfere and drown out the beat. Memories sweep in. Cereal together for breakfast. Sitting on the couch and watching movies, eating popcorn and binge-watching reality shows. Apologizing over pizza. And in the wake of this new tune, I hear other songs I once knew, other voices. Love and work and friendship. Melody and harmony, songs that called me to waltz, to stomp, to soar and stretch. How could I have forgotten them—the love, the need, the rage, the mundane passion of my life before the dance?

The perfect, mesmerizing music pounds at me again, stronger now, and my soul leans toward it. It would be so easy to be lost to the rhythm.

But there is something else pounding at me too, an urgency dragging me back to where I belong. I force my feet out of step, fall. I wrench from my partner's grasp.

And I crawl. If I stand, my feet will draw me back. That is not my song, not my dance, not my purpose.

I have different tunes to dance to.

Story Notes

"Unknown"

A tribute to caves and grottos and dangerous places. Reading, writing, and life in general feel like this sometimes—a step into the unknown, which hopefully holds treasure to go with the danger.

"Unspeakable Sweaters"

First published in *A Grimm Ever After: A Collection of Urban Fantasy Fairy Tales* (2022).

Based loosely on "The Six Swans" and other similar tales. I've always loved variations on this tale, especially exploring the power the sister wields despite her silence and imagining the life of the brother with the wing.

"The Elf and the Fisherman"

First published in *Unsightly* (2025).

Based on folk tales of helpful elves, including "The Elves and the Shoemaker," and tales of fishermen's wild catches, including "The Fisherman and His Wife." I think we often don't know what we actually want—and maybe we need to find more joy in what we get.

"Diamonds and Pearls"

Based on Perrault's "Diamonds and Toads." My reading of fairy tales and folklore has convinced me that fairies are Very Bad at giving gifts. Coughing up gemstones every time you speak? No thank you. But I love the main character of this type of tale so much. I've got a novel in the works for her and the "Six Swans" brother.

"Forged in Iron and Blood"

First published in *Deep Magic Ezine* and then collected in *Deep Magic: Volume II* (2024).

Based on the common folklore of fae creatures having an aversion to iron. I was drawn to the idea of Lina as someone who cared deeply about peace, enough to make a great deal of sacrifice to keep it.

"The Nanny Job"

First published in *Snow White: 11 Retellings of the Popular Fairy Tale: A Timeless Tales Collection* (2019).

Based on "Snow White," "Jack and the Beanstalk," "Little Red Riding Hood," and "Goldilocks and the Three Bears," all thrown together and shaken very hard. Who doesn't fall at least a little in love with a guy who owns a food truck?

"Daughters of Sea"

Based on "The Little Mermaid." The original tale is so bittersweet. I like to envision her riding the winds and having joy in it, but I'm not sure where or if her story ever truly ends.

"Some Restrictions Apply"

Based on tales of genies in lamps, like "Aladdin." Also based on a firm belief that even magic has bounds—and sometimes a few more bounds than we'd really like.

"Song and Storm"
First published in *Deep Magic: Volume III* (2025).
Based on siren tales. I love stories where a villain makes the choice to not be villainous, and I wanted to tell a story of love both familial and romantic and how it shapes lives.

"The Promise of Snow"
First published in *Love Undefined* (2017).
Based loosely on selkie and shapeshifter stories, along with tales of magic portals and fairy rings. What if the portal changed who you were? What if you couldn't get back? And, most of all, what is the meaning of home?

"The Candlemaker"
Based on "Godfather Death," a story that fundamentally annoys me. I wanted a better outcome.

"Breadcrumbs"
First published in *Unspun: A Collection of Tattered Fairy Tales* (2018).
Based on "Hansel and Gretel" and a hint of "Snow White." This story, along with *Unsightly*, cemented my love of retelling fairy tales. Writing this story for *Unspun* was exactly the gift I needed—and a gift that continues to bless me. (Thanks, Kathy! And thanks, Sarah, for getting me involved in this project!) Regarding the story itself, I had never before thought about what life must have been like for Gretel after she and Hansel came home. I wanted to explore that aspect of her life.

"The Cinderella Plan"
Based on "Cinderella." And also my general feelings about the lack of economic accountability in fairy tale settings.

"A Selection of Documents…"

Based on a wide array of fairy tale tropes—clever third children, the "normal" child, girls who can talk to animals, magic mirrors, dragons and ogres and fairy tale monsters, princes who aren't very princely, wooden stirring spoons. Also based on the idea that many of us probably got a lot of yearbook notes that said things like "Keep smiling! Let's hang out sometime!" We may have felt invisible or unknown or unneeded as teens. We may feel inadequate to our tasks as adults. We are neither.

"Wolfskin"

First published in *Unsightly* (2025).

Based on selkie stories, though I'm drawn more to creatures of the forest than of the water. I'm also drawn to questions of forgiveness and redemption. What can be forgiven? What does true penitence look like?

"Siren's Younger Sister"

First published in *A Little Fantasy Everywhere* (2024).
Based on siren stories. And also ridiculous reality shows.

"Spun from Linen and Lies"

Based loosely on "Rumpelstiltskin" (more like a raging game of telephone where "Rumpelstiltskin" got really muddled along the way), along with fae folklore. After I wrote "Forged in Iron and Blood," I was surprised by the number of people who wanted a sequel. I think there was something special about Lina—her sacrifice, her quiet power, her age, her secrets. Also, Seelah. And her baskets. I love that these characters who are much older than the average fairy tale MC get to go out and have adventures. I imagine them traveling and getting into and out of trouble for years to come.

"Sharp and Pointy Teeth"

Based on portal fantasy, silliness, and my brother's love of boxes. Also, I reached what is possibly the pinnacle of coolness when my daughter decided to dress up as Bitey Box for Book Week at school.

"To Dance with the Fae"

Based on fae folklore. I'm intrigued by the idea of fairy circles and disappearing and losing time—there's something interesting and scary about coming back to a different world if you get lost in the fae one. But I am drawn most to the idea of staying, of choosing a life that isn't lost in the whirl and enchantment but instead grounded in the real. I think that's where true magic exists.

Acknowledgments and Kickstarter Thank Yous

It's hard to know where to start. So many people have influenced and contributed to the stories in this collection.

I am grateful to my children, who inspire me, brainstorm with me, listen to me whinge about plot points, and happily do their own thing while I write. They are also tremendously good at snuggles. I love you more than all the food in all the fridges in all the world.

My husband, Brice, who holds down the fort while I do deadlines and other creative chaos. The process of putting this collection together came when we were overrun with so many other obstacles, particularly related to my own health. He repeatedly came through so I could try to hold myself together, and he was a shoulder to cry on every time I couldn't. He continues to provide strength, loving reality checks, and silly dances to charm me out of my bad moods. In a world of pigeons, you are a bird of paradise.

The Glorious Kathy Cowley, who helped me on my Kickstarter journey, talked me through various crises, and provided brilliant feedback, along with about a thousand other things. You deserve the Double Gloucester wheel of cheese that they chase down Cooper's Hill every year, but without any broken bones.

My amazing writing critique group, Whitney, David, and Jake. We all have been through the wringer lately, but you continue in your support and friendship. You read my back cover copy until I want to throw my computer out the window. You also help me figure out where the doors, streams, and pockets are. May you always remember how to spell coooridddieoor.

Laura, for all the nights spent watching *Avatar: The Last Airbender*. I'm sorry about Jet. Jane, for being my fellow outlaw. Cesia, for the times we've gotten to sit together and watch the child chaos unfold. Marneen, for bringing meals and advice and sisterly love. K-onna, for continuing to lend a little inspiration from above. Dawn, Kem, West, Makani, for your support, prayers, and occasional sibling obnoxiousness that translates as love. Elissa, for all the ways your friendship has held me together.

Finally, thank you to so many amazing people who helped and supported my Kickstarter project, allowing me to bring this short story collection to life. You are an unexpected treasure gleaming in a dark cave. Alexandra Corrsin, Alexis Hope, Amanda Bruce, AndieRae, Anna Drenth, Anniebelle, Ariane Beauparlant, Ash D., Becky Brucato, Brigette Estrada, Carol MacLennan-Gonzales, Cassandra G., Charity West, Cherelle H., Chris C., Christy S., Corina, Corrie Pelc, Cortney Babcock, Daphne Tatum, Denne, E. R. Paskey, Elissa Meyer, Elleemmenno, Emerald Bruce, Emily Yuyuenyongwatana, Emma Shirley, Emma Van Arnam, Erin Davis, Erin Main, Gabrielle Landi, Gwen, Hannah Lozano, Heather Dow, J. L. Hendricks, Jeff Wheeler, Joyce Stay, Kara Lindstrom, Kara Malachi, Karina Krogh, Kat Vroman, Katelyn Hester, Katherine Malloy, Kelli Higley, Kelly Adams, Kerry Mitchell, Kyo Carter, Larisa I., Larissa Green, Laura Cutler, Lauren E. W. Johnson, Liana, Lisa Firke, Liz Busby, Lorien Cord, Lynden Wade, M., M. A. Boslow, Madelyn S., Makani Mason, my indispensable youngest older sister Marneen, Megan Lewis, Michelle Hutchins, MichelleG, Nadya Houston, Nicole Pfau, Nicole Wilkes Goldberg and James Goldberg, Nicole Wright, Olivia Singletary, Pauline Beltran, my Taylorsville bestie

Rachel Kummer, Rebecca Buchanan, Rebecca P., Rebecca Wyse, the ever-fantastic Regina Verow, RLS, Samantha Newberry, Sarah Chow, Sarah Blake Johnson, Sariah "the best college roommate ever" Reeder, Shavon Bledsoe, Sheena, Stacey Andrews, Stephan and the interstellar Dawn, Stephanie F., Stephen Sagers, Sunny Ryan, Tammy Bigelow, Tamson Farnsworth, Tara Lytle, Terri L., Terry Juell French, Tess, The Yiwis, Theric Jepson, Todd and Melissa Jones, Trista R. Whitaker, ValerieAnne, Verity, Ysabel Jardine, and others unnamed.

If you, fair reader, are perusing these acknowledgments and think you belong here, you probably do. I probably wandered into a fairy ring and forgot to include you. Please feel free to let me know in a sternly worded email. I will read it, be reminded of your incredibleness and feel properly abashed that I forgot to include you, and… probably forget to reply.

About the Author

Jeanna Mason Stay once had tomatoes thrown at her while she was reciting poetry, and honestly, it's all been uphill from there. When she's not being pelted with vegetables, she enjoys avoiding dishes and laundry, sewing costume projects that force her to learn new skills, and playing board games. Jeanna loves a good happily-ever-after in book, movie, or song, but her favorite is in real life: she and her husband have been happily-ever-aftering for the last twenty years, including in Maryland, Australia, and Utah. They have four children who've been raised on a steady diet of fantasy novels, math trivia, and word nerdery, so naturally they are delightful.

Jeanna writes in a variety of genres, but rom com, fantasy/fairy tale, and ghost stories are her favorites.

www.ingramcontent.com/pod-product-compliance
Lightning Source LLC
LaVergne TN
LVHW041759060526
838201LV00046B/1053